神のみる夢

合田 和厚

The
Dreams
of
God

Yasuhiro Goda

観客の少ない映画館で、ゆったりと好きな映画を観れる事はとても嬉しいものです。しかし、それがサーカスだったらあなたは映画を観るように心を集中する事が出来るでしょうか。

まばらな客席から、楽しみにしていたサーカスを観る時あなたの心には、理由を探すのが悲しくなるような何かが、込み上げてくるかも知れません。

生きている喜びを、あなただけの中から探り出すのではなくて、共に生きている全てのものからも感じる事が出来るなら、どんなに素晴らしい事でしょうか。

本作は、心の世界を、あなたから、愛する人、自然、神、宇宙、未来まで、時空を超えて拡大させていければとの願いをこめて執筆しました。

すぐれた絵や音楽は感動する為の理屈などいらないものです。感動を呼び起こす言葉など必要とせずダイレクトに心に広がってきます。

それは、まるで、初めて恋をした時のように、心をときめかせるのです。

「神のみる夢」もあなたの心に少しでも無理なく届く事が出来れば、これにまさる喜びはありません。

合田 和厚

Sitting back and watching your favorite movie in a cinema with a small audience brings great joy. If it was a circus, however, would you be able to stay focused as much as a movie?

A sentiment with a sad cause may well up in your heart when you watch a long-awaited circus in a sparse auditorium.

It would be so wonderful if you could find the joy of living not only for your own sake but also to share it with everything that coexists.

I wrote this collection of poems, wishing for the readers to expand their hearts beyond time and space, to their loved ones, nature, God, the universe and the future.

You do not need a reason to be moved by wonderful paintings and music. They just directly reach us and expand in our heart without words to arouse sensation. Such excitement is just like the first time you fall in love.

It would be my utmost pleasure if *The Dreams of God* reaches your heart as naturally as possible.

Yasuhiro Goda

目次　　Contents

神のみる夢　*The Dreams of God*

CHAPTER 1
月　*CONSCIENCE*   12

神の像　*ILLUSION*   14
月　*CONSCIENCE*   18
流れる水　*HEART*   20
こぼれる涙　*FREEDOM*   22
鏡　*SECRET*   24

CHAPTER 2
自我　*FOOL*   26

自我　*FOOL*   28
祈り　*DESIRE*   30
草原の花　*WAVE*   34
知性と欲望と悪魔　*INTELLIGENCE*   36

CHAPTER 3
愛する事　*WORDS*   42

愛する事　*WORDS*   44
愛と欲望　*BLUE*   48
別離　*FOREVER*   52
存在　*GRATITUDE*   54
偶然の幸福　*GENTLY*   58
マッチの火　*SUNLIGHT*   62

CHAPTER 4

自然 *GOD*   64

  海 *MOTHER*   66
  海のゆくえ *REINCARNATION*   68
  空（くう）*LOVE*   72
  空（くう）II *BREATH*   76
  聖者 *BIG RIVER*   78
  自然 *GOD*   80
  自然（かみ）の生命（いのち）*COSMOS*   82

CHAPTER 5

ルネッサンスの予感 *OLD & NEW*   84

  ルネッサンスの予感 *OLD & NEW*   86
  魂と肉体 *RULE*   92
  記憶 *POSSESSION*   98
  憑依 *QUARK*   100
  宇宙と時間 *0×60=60*   104

CHAPTER 6

小さな恐竜 *HUMAN BEINGS*   108

  言葉 *ISOLATION*   110
  超能力 *MELODY*   112
  小さな恐竜 *HUMAN BEINGS*   114
  タイムマシン *NO FUTURE*   120
  タンポポ *SPRING*   126

CHAPTER 7
光のごとく *MISTY*   128

光のごとく *MISTY*   130
一瞬の彼方 *SHADOW*   132
夢 *STORY*   134
ぶどうの房 *A PIECE OF HEART*   136

CHAPTER 1
The Moon *CONSCIENCE*   142

Statues of God *ILLUSION*   144
The Moon *CONSCIENCE*   148
Flowing Water *HEART*   150
Tears Falling *FREEDOM*   152
Mirror *SECRET*   154

CHAPTER 2
The Ego *FOOL*   156

The Ego *FOOL*   158
Prayers *DESIRE*   160
Flowers in a Meadow *WAVE*   164
Intellect, Desires and Devils *INTELLIGENCE*   166

CHAPTER 3
To Love *WORDS*   172

To Love *WORDS*   174
Love and Desire *BLUE*   178
Separation *FOREVER*   182
Existence *GRATITUDE*   184
Happiness by Chance *GENTLY*   188
Match Flame *SUNLIGHT*   192

CHAPTER 4
Nature GOD   194

The Sea MOTHER   196
The Sea's Destination REINCARNATION   198
The Air LOVE   202
The Air II BREATH   206
Saints BIG RIVER   208
Nature GOD   210
Life of Nature COSMOS   212

CHAPTER 5
Anticipation of a Renaissance OLD & NEW   214

Anticipation of a Renaissance OLD & NEW   216
Soul and Body RULE   222
Memories POSSESSION   228
Possession QUARK   230
The Universe and Time 0×60=60   234

CHAPTER 6
Little Dinosaurs HUMAN BEINGS   238

Words ISOLATION   240
Supernatural Power MELODY   242
Little Dinosaurs HUMAN BEINGS   244
Time Machine NO FUTURE   250
Dandelions SPRING   256

CHAPTER 7
As It Were Light *MISTY*   258

    As It Were Light *MISTY*   260
    Beyond the Moment *SHADOW*   262
    Dream *STORY*   264
    Bunch of Grapes *A PIECE OF HEART*   266

CHAPTER 1

月

CONSCIENCE

遠くから陽が射してきて

僕は待ち焦がれていたものに

逢えそうな気がする

神の像　ILLUSION

あなたが
心から湧き上がる信仰心から
真の神の姿を探し求める為
世界中の　聖地　寺院　教会を旅しようと決心して
ある日　旅立つのです

一年　二年と過ぎ
数多くの経典を学び
数えきれぬ程の　神の絵画や彫刻を見てもなお神を求める心はやまず
あなたは　さらに次の寺院を訪ねようとします

けれども　手持ちの金は底を尽き
宿もとれぬばかりか　食物さえ買う事も出来ません

精根尽き果て
あなたは　ついに旅の途中で倒れてしまうのです
目も見えず　意識も薄れ
「死人のように」道端にころがっているのです
やせ衰え　ボロボロになったあなたに　気付く人は誰もいないのです

その時
一人の男があなたの側へ来て　手を取ってくれるのです
あなたを抱き上げ　彼の粗末な寝床まで運ぶと
食べかけのパンと水を　あなたに分けてくれるのです

彼は　定まった職も無くその日暮らしの貧しき者でした
おまけに　彼は信仰を持たぬばかりか
神の事など考えた事もない　無学で無教養な者でした

勿論　彼には　あなたが神を探して旅をし
行き倒れになっている事など　思いもよりません
ただ　道に倒れているあなたを見過ごせず　手厚く介抱してくれるのです

彼の腕の中　乾いた唇に水を飲ませてもらいながら
あなたは虚ろな目で彼を見て　こう思うのです

「神のおかげだ」と
「神が私の為に　この哀れな男を使い　私の生命を救ってくれたのだ」と

あなたに　水やパンを与えてくれる彼の姿など目に入らぬように
数々の寺院や教会で見た　神の絵画や彫刻を思い浮かべては
ひたすら礼を言い続けるのです

しかし　あなたが祈り続けた絵画の神や彫刻の神は
あなたが倒れた時に　一滴の水でも与えてくれたでしょうか

何よりもあなたの生命を救う為に　必要だったのは
無学で信仰を持たぬ　彼が与えてくれたパンと水ではなかったでしょうか
けれども　あなたはそれに気付こうとはしないのです

真の神の姿は　あなたを介抱してくれた　彼の優しさの中にあるのです

神は

あなたを道端から抱き起こしてくれた　彼の腕であり
あなたの乾いた唇に水を与えてくれた　彼の手そのものなのです

そして
あなたの生命を助けようとする
彼の思いやりの心と　思いやりの仕草　それが神の姿なのです

神は

人の優しさと　思いやりの中にあるのです

あなたが全てのものに対して
感謝の心を持つ事が出来るなら

神の姿を

人ばかりでなく　全てのものの恵みの中にも発見出来るのです

普段　気にも留めなかった衣服　毎日の食物　住まいに対し
感謝の心を持つ事が
神の恵みを知る一番の早道である事を知るでしょう

それは　決して動かぬ絵画や彫刻の神からは
得られない愛と喜びを　あなたにもたらす事でしょう

長い時間を費やし
長い距離を歩いた　あなたの神への旅は
ここで初めて　終わりとなるのです

あなたは　もう
神を求めて　多くの寺院や教会を旅する必要はないのです

神は

あなたが何処にいようと　何をしようと
あなたのすぐそば
それはあなたの心の中に　見い出す事が出来るのですから

月　CONSCIENCE

コップがあなたの肉体なら
コップに注がれる水は　あなたの魂であり　生命そのものと言えるでしょう

神は　あなたという水面に映る月の如く　あなたの心にゆらめいているのです

コップ　すなわちあなたの肉体が
粗末なものでも　高価なものでも
映る月の姿は　同じ色と同じ形をしています
小さくとも　プール位の大きなものでも
水面に映る月は　一つだけであるように

神は全ての生命あるものに　分け隔てなくその恵みを与えているのです

弱い者にも強い者にも　醜い者にも美しい者にも
貧しき者にも豊かな者にも　愚かな者にもそうでない者にも
その姿をありのままに　とどめているはずなのです

水は
純粋で透明な程
月の輝きを　水中深くまで映すように

あなたの魂も素直で　潔らかなものである程
あなたは　真実の神の姿を
魂の奥深くまでくっきりと　見い出す事が出来るでしょう

水面が
穏やかで波立ちが少ない程　月の姿をありのまま映し出すように

あなたが　人生に愛の意味を見い出し
憂いの時も　悲しみの時も
感謝と思いやりを忘れぬ　優しき人なら

あなたは自らの魂の中に　神の姿を見る事が出来るでしょう

濁った水は
月の輝きを　水中深く映す事はできません

あなたが喜びを持てず　人としての良心を忘れ
我欲だけに捕われるなら　あなたに神を見る事は出来ないでしょう

波立つ水面は
月の姿を　歪んだものにしてしまいます

あなたが悲しみや憂いに　心を痛めたり
憎しみや怒りばかりに　捕われるなら
あなたの魂も波立ちざわめき
あなたは神の姿も　歪んだものに見えてくるでしょう

神は降り注ぐ　月の光のように
誰にも平等に　その愛を与えているのです

そしてあなたは　月を映す水であり
あなたの魂が　良心と呼べるものであるなら

神は
鏡に映るあなた自身であり　あなたと一つになった　愛の姿そのものなのです

流れる水　HEART

　流れる水は　新鮮で瑞々しく　清らかで美しいものです

　人は　その水を浴びてみたいと思い
　水を飲む事に　何のためらいも持たないでしょう

　しかし　流れる水も
　一度その動きを止め　流れる事のなくなった溜り水となれば
　時と共に　濁り　淀み　苔むし　微生物やボウフラの住み家となります
　そうなれば　人は決してその水を飲みたいとも浴びたいとも思わなくなるのです

　心も　また
　流れる水の如く絶えず動き　変化してこそ
　生き生きとした　美しいものでいられるのです

　たとえば一滴の雨水は
　地上に落ち　海に流れ着くまでの間に
　木の葉のしずく　岩間を流れるせせらぎ
　田畑を潤す小川　大地を悠々と流れる大河へとその姿を次々と変えていきます

　人の心も同様に
　この世に誕生してから　死して母なる神の元へ帰っていくまでの間に
　多くの変化を遂げるのです

　喜び　悲しみ　希望　絶望　怒り　優しさ　恐れ　勇気
　善　悪　愛　嫌悪　安心　不安　嫉妬　得意　友情……
　人の心は千差万別

様々にその姿や色合いを変えながら　豊かになっていくのです
水が　絶えず流れ続ける事で　その美しさを保つように
心も　絶えず変化し続ける事で　その美しさを保つのです

それはまるで血液が
体内を絶えず流れ続ける事で
新陳代謝を行ない　生命を維持していく様にも似ています

血液の流れが肉体の生命を保つように
心が常に変化する事は　あなたが生きている証とも言えるでしょう

朝顔の花が　水の色で花びらを赤や紫に染めるように
人も心によって　幸せ色にも不幸の色にも染まるのです

あなたの心が　自分の喜びだけに執着し
他人の悩みや不幸を　思いやれないものであれば
あなたの心は　毒を含んだ溜り水と言えるでしょう

毒水に咲く花は　誰からも愛されない孤独で寂しい花となるでしょう

しかし　あなたの心が
喜びや悲しみなどの変化を恐れぬ　強くて素直なものであれば
あなたは生き生きとして　健康で誰からも愛される幸福な人になるでしょう

いつも新鮮で清らかな水に咲く　美しい花と言えるのです

こぼれる涙　FREEDOM

わずかな時間でさえ　人をコントロールする為に
あなたは絶えず神経を使い
緊張から解放される事がないでしょう

まして　自分の心をコントロールする為には
莫大なエネルギーと忍耐を
必要とすると思っているのではないでしょうか

心をコントロールする為には
感情を消せば良いのでしょうか

それとも　心を
強引に変化させれば良いのでしょうか
あなたの考えている心のコントロールとは

あなたが　自分自身でなくなる事ではないでしょうか

　　湧き起こる恐怖を　あなたはどうすればいいのでしょうか
　　こぼれ落ちる涙を　あなたはどうすればいいのでしょうか
　　かえがたい笑顔を　あなたはどうすればいいのでしょうか
　　こみ上げる愛しさを　あなたはどうすればいいのでしょうか

自然に湧き出る感情に　逆らう必要などないのです
喜びも　悲しみも　苦しみも　優しさも
感情の全ては
あなたの心に自然に湧き上がる　生命の証と言えるものなのです

あなたは　ただ人として
素直な心に従えば良いのです

素直な心とは
あなた以外の人の心を　思いやるという事
他のものへの思いやりを　忘れないという事
それは　あなたの良心に従う事でもあるのです

だからあなたの心が　常に良心と呼べるものなら
あなたは自分の心をコントロールする事など　考える必要もないのです

　　自然に眠り　自然に夢み　自然に目覚め
　　自然に笑い　自然に泣き
　　自然に愛し　自然に愛され……

　　自然に生きる事の喜び

　　そのなんと素晴らしい事か

あなたが良心を持ち　人として素直に生きるなら
あなたは晴天の空の如く
誰からも愛され望まれる人となるでしょう

あなたは自分の心を　自由に解き放てさえすれば良いのです

鏡　SECRET

あなたは　自分の怒った顔を
鏡に映して見ても　恐いとは思わないでしょう
それは自分の顔であるし　あなたは怒っている自分を知っているから

他の人に　あなたの怒っている顔を
いきなり見せたら恐いと思うでしょう
それは自分の顔でないし　あなたが怒っている事を知らなかったから

あなたが　自分の泣いている顔を
鏡に映しても　驚いたりしないでしょう
それはあなたの顔であるし　あなたは泣いている事を知っているから

他の人に　あなたの泣いている顔を
いきなり見せたなら　きっと驚く事でしょう
それは自分の顔ではないし　あなたが泣いている事も知らなかったから

しかし神に　あなたの怒っている顔を見せても
泣き顔を見せても　神は恐いとも思わないし驚く事もないでしょう

なぜなら
あなた自身が神の化身であり　神はいつもあなたと共にいて
あなたが人知れず　こっそり泣いている事も全て知っているのですから

CHAPTER 2

自我
FOOL

都会の雑踏の中

君だけしか見なかった

夏の夜

自我　*FOOL*

光の中で傘をさすと
傘の下には　小さな影が一つ出来ます

傘をたたむと
影は跡片もなく消え去り　あとは無限の光だけとなります

海の水は　小さなコップに汲めば手に持つ事も出来ます
海に流せばコップの水は一瞬にして　広大な海と化すのです

生命ある存在に宿る魂も
死すれば　神という無限の魂とひとつになるのです

ところが私達は
姿　形の違う肉体を持つ事で「自我」を作り上げました

自分と他のもの
実はひとつである事を　見失ってしまったのです

私達の肉体は傘であり　コップと同じなのです

神から見れば「自我」とは

晴れた日に傘をさすような
また船上で　海水を小さなコップに入れて大事に持っているような

無意味な事であり
無限の光　広大な海を見ようともしない　愚かな事と言えるのです

祈り　DESIRE

　未開のジャングルでは　神を奉るのに
　魚や獣ばかりでなく　時として人間でさえも
　その生け贄とされる事があります

　先進国に住む私達は
　決してその神の信者になろうとは　思わないはずです
　いやそれどころか　神とも思わないでしょう

　しかし　ジャングルに住む彼等には
　何よりも崇高な神と信じられているのです

　彼等の祈りの中では
　争いや戦いでの勝利を願う事がしばしばあります

　敵対する部族民を殺害したり
　村を焼き払うような祈りも行なわれるのです
　そのような彼等の祈りは　冷酷かつ残忍なものです

　そして　彼等の信ずる神は
　生け贄を持ち　奉る彼等のために
　他の者を傷つける願いを聞き入れるのです

　それは　もはや神ではなく　悪魔としか言いようがありません

比べようもなく　文明の発達した現代社会に住む私達にとって
それが正しい祈りでない事
正しい神への祈りでない事は　容易に理解出来るはずです

でも　もう一度考えてみて下さい
人の祈りは千差万別なものです

あなたの唱える祈りの中に
未開のジャングルで　行なわれているような
悪魔的な祈りも　数多く存在しているのではないでしょうか

あなたは　その願いの中に
他人を思いやる心を　失ってはいないでしょうか

今からほんの数十年前　第二次世界大戦の時

今の文明国
いやその時すでに文明国と呼ばれた国民達は
自国が勝つ為　結果的にせよ
相手国を滅ぼすような祈りを　唱えてはいなかったでしょうか

それは　形こそ違え
ジャングルでの祈りと　同じものであったと言えないでしょうか

今　あなたが祈る心の中に
自分の願いが叶うなら
他の者はどうなってもいい　という思いがないと言えるでしょうか

もし　あなたの願いや祈りの中に
人より幸せになりたい　人より裕福になりたいというような

すなわち　あなたの願いの中に
「人より……」という気持ちがあるのなら
あなたの祈りは　正しい神への祈りとは言えないでしょう

あなたは　自分の人生の喜びを
人と比べなければ得る事が出来ない　愚かな人と言えるでしょう

食べている物を　美味しいと感じていても
隣の人が　自分より美味しそうな物を食べていると
突然　自分の食べている物を不味く感じたり

友人の家が　豪華で広々としているのを見ると
自分の家や　今の生活がみじめに思えたり

恋人から貰ったプレゼントを
友人が貰ったプレゼントと比較して
高級でない事や高価でない事を　不幸だと思ったりした事はないでしょうか

自分より不幸な人を見て安心し
自分より幸福な人を見て落胆し

不幸な人を思いやる心を忘れ
自分は　不幸だと決めつけてはいないでしょうか

個人の利己的な願いの為に
他の者を犠牲にするような祈りを　唱えてはいないでしょうか

その利己的な願いを叶えるのは　神ではなく悪魔なのです

悪魔に祈る行為は
腹黒く欲の深い人に　願い事をするのと同じで
あなたは叶えられた祈りの　何倍もの代償を払わなければならないでしょう

祈るあなたの心が
思いやりもなく身勝手なものだけであれば　そこに神はいないでしょう

しかしあなたの願いが　人と比べるものではなく
そしてあなたの祈りに　平和を愛する心が込められているなら

どんなに些細な事でも　どんなに困難な事でも
どんなに奇跡的な事でも
あなたの願いは叶えられ　神から祝福してもらえるものとなるでしょう

草原の花　WAVE

草原に咲く花は美しい
あなたは陽の中　咲き誇る花を見るのがとても好きです

その花の美しさを　いつも自分のものにしたいと
花を摘み取るのです

しかし　手にした花に　生命の息吹はなく
風にそよぐ花の美しさは　失われているのです

蝶を追い　野原を駆け回る子馬は
まるで無邪気な天使のように見えます

あなたは
子馬を捕えて柵の中に入れるのです

しかし　捕えた子馬に
天使のような目は　すでに失く
生命力あふれる美しさのかけらも　残っていないのです

あなたには　愛する人がいて
その人の何気ない仕草や　小さな微笑みに　胸ときめかせ
聞き取れぬ声に　言葉を思い描きます

あなたは
その人を独占したいと　一緒に暮らし始めるでしょう

それでもなお
もっともっと　独占したいと思うあなたは
愛する人の何気ない仕草や
ほんの小さな微笑みに　胸をときめかす事もなく
聞き取れぬ声に　言葉を思い描く事もなくなるのです

知性と欲望と悪魔　*INTELLIGENCE*

獣の行動パターンの殆どを決定するのは
食欲　睡眠欲　性欲であり

それは生命を守り　子孫を絶やさぬ為の基本的欲望で
決して知性から生じたものではありません

人間の行動を決定するのは
基本的欲望もさることながら
知性によって生ずる　様々な欲望による場合が多いのです

人間の行動が
獣と比べようがない程　複雑かつ奇妙なのは
人間が　獣とは比較にならない程の知性を持つからです

そして
その知性から生じた欲望は　数限りなく
次から次へと湧いて来るのです

あなたがTVを見る
車のコマーシャルを見て　新しい車が欲しいと思うでしょう
ドラマを見て　このヒロインのように　生きてみたいと思うでしょう

あなたが街を歩いている
すれ違う恋人たちを見て　あなたは恋がしたいと思うでしょう
素敵な街並みを見て　ここに住みたいと思うでしょう

基本的は欲望は
人間誰しも生まれた時から備わっているもので
それは純粋な肉体の欲望であり

その満足の度合は　肉体の満足感として
自然に得る事の出来るものなのです

しかし　知性から生ずる欲望

すなわち
他の何かを知る事により生じる欲望は
一人一人の心でしか　その満足の度合を量る事が出来ないのです

まして人は　一つの欲望を叶える事により
さらに　大きな欲望を生む事になるのです

たとえば　あなたが望みの洋服を手に入れたとします
その時は満足しても　自分より素敵な服を着ている人がいれば

あなたは　その服を着る事さえ恥ずかしく感じ
また新しい服を欲しいと思うでしょう

たとえば　あなたが家を建てたとします
最初の一、二年は　希望の家を持てた事で満足しても

三年も過ぎる頃になると　もっと広い家が欲しくなるでしょう

あなたは　今の家では満足出来なくなり
新たなる家への欲望が　日増しに膨れ上がっていくのです

人間の欲望に限りがないのは

人間には知る能力があり
絶えず新しいものへの興味から生じる欲望には限りがないからです

しかし知性は
現在の満足を不満に変えてしまう　恐ろしい力とも言えるのです

人の心は　とても貪欲なものです

読んだり聞いたりしたものを　実際に見てみたいと思い
見たものは触れてみたいと思い　触れたものは所有したいと思い
所有したものは独占したいと思うのです

そして独占した後は
手に入れたおもちゃにすぐ飽きた子供が　次のおもちゃを欲しがるように
新たな欲望を生み出すのです

歴史上に見る数々の戦争も
個人や国家の欲望を
叶える為のものではなかったでしょうか

人間の過ちには　知性から湧きでた欲望が
災いしている場合が　非常に多いと言えるでしょう

奴隷制度や身分制度があった　古代から中世において
時の権力者や　それに準ずる者以外は
知性を持つ事は許されず
支配者達に反発する事もなく　労働へと駆り立てられました

戦士達は　戦う理由も知らぬまま　戦場で死んでいきました

人間らしさとは
基本的な欲望以外にも　様々な欲望を持つ事の出来る素晴らしさにあるのですが

奴隷や戦士達には
知る権利さえ与えられず
生命を守るという基本的な欲望でさえ　充分叶えられたとは言えないでしょう

そして
誰もが自由に　知る権利を与えられている現代
新たな不幸が人間を襲うようになりました

それは
嵐のような目まぐるしい情報が駆け巡る中で
人間の知性が　かつてなかった程の速さで
新しい欲望を生み落としている事です

多くのものを知る事により　多くの不満を作り出し
自分と他人を比べては　不幸を感じ

ある者は叶わぬ欲望に生命を捨て　ある者は過ちを犯すのです

欲望の善悪を問うもの
それがなければ　人間の行動は欲望の赴くまま

目的を達成する為には
手段を選ばない非情なものとなってしまいます

それは再び悲惨な戦争を生み
人が人を傷つける事になるのです

知性と欲望だけが支配する社会
それは　ひどく悪魔的な世界と言えるでしょう

悪魔は
知性に富み行動はすばやくひどく合理的でさえあるのです

しかし　悪魔に唯一つないもの
それは　理性なのです

理性こそ
欲望の善悪を自らに問いかける　偉大なる力　と言えるでしょう

CHAPTER 3

愛する事
WORDS

冬の前　澄んだ空

　　永遠の時に値する君との時間

愛する事　WORDS

　あなたが

　悲しみを知るのは　あなたに心があるから
　喜びを知るのは　あなたに心があるから

　しかし　心の場所を聞かれたら　あなたには答える事が出来ません

　なぜなら

　心は　思考する場所ではなく
　心は　素直に湧き上がってくるものだから
　心とは　動かぬ石のように不変なものではなく
　心とは　流れる水の如く変化するものだから

　あなたは

　心を見つける手だてが　解らないというかも知れません
　心を見つける手だてなど　知らなくていいのです

　心は

　あなた自身だから
　あなたが　愛によって生命を授かったように
　心もまた　愛によって創造されたものだから

　心に

　浮かぶ全ての思いは
　愛なくして語れぬものばかり　全ての言葉は愛から生まれたもの

たとえば美しさ　美しさから愛を知るのではないのです
愛する事で　美しさを知るのです

たとえば勇気　勇気を持つ事で愛を知るのではないのです
愛する事で　勇気を知るのです

たとえば悲しみ　悲しみにより愛を知るのではないのです
愛する事で　悲しみを知るのです

たとえば情け　情けがあるから愛を知るのではないのです
愛する事で　情けを知るのです

たとえば優しさ　優しくする事で愛を知るのではないのです
愛する事で　優しさを知るのです

愛する事で勇気を知り
愛する事で恐れを知り
愛する事で喜びを知り
愛する事で苦しみを知り
愛する事で愛を知る

愛する事で子を知り
愛する事で親を知り
愛する事で友を知り
愛する事で恋を知り
愛する事で神を知る

心の全ての思いも
世にある全ての言葉の意味も　愛がその基準となるのです

　　　憎しみは人を愛せぬ言葉
　　　悲しみは自分を愛せぬ言葉

愛するなら

言葉は　心に無理なく届くもの
悟りでさえ　真理でさえ　神でさえ　愛する事で知る事が出来るのです

愛と欲望　*BLUE*

　あなたは　自分の人生を愛したいはず

　人生を愛せる事こそ
　何ものにも勝る幸福である事を知っています

　人生を愛する為には
　様々な欲望が　叶わなければいけないと考えて
　あなたは湧き起こる欲望を　満たそうとするでしょう

　金銭欲　名誉欲
　独占欲　所有欲　様々な肉欲の数々……

　あなたは
　とりとめもなく湧き起こる欲望が　叶う時こそ
　人生を最高に愛せる時と信じて　一生懸命になるでしょう

　しかし
　欲望を満たす事が不可能だと解ると
　あなたは欲望を
　いや人生すら呪うようになるのです

　あなたは
　自分を愛するあまり　人生を不幸なものと感じてしまうのです

　自分を愛する事と
　人生を愛する事は　似て否なるものです

　自分だけを愛する者は　愛の意味さえ解らなくなるのです

あなたは愛と欲望とを　混同してはいないでしょうか

あなたが恋人を思う気持ちは
独占欲だったり　所有欲だったりしてはいないでしょうか

あなたは
愛も欲望と同じように

叶わなければ　意味がないと思ってはいないでしょうか
叶わなければ　辛いだけのものと思ってはいないでしょうか

だから　愛する事に対しても
欲望と同じように見返りを期待して　臆病になってはいないでしょうか

欲望は
叶う事であなたのものになり　叶ったとたんに消えていくものです

愛は　たとえ叶わなくとも
愛する事だけで　永遠にあなたのものとなるのです

　　愛とは　　愛される事でも
　　　　　　愛してもらおうという思いでもなく

　　愛とは　　愛する事だけ　ただそれだけ

愛は　愛する事だけで　立派にあなたのものとなるのです

あなたが
人生を最高に愛せる時は
真実の愛を見つけた時といえるでしょう

真実の愛は
自分の欲望さえ忘れる程　自分以外の何かを愛する事

それは
自分の人生を愛せる事となるのです

たとえば　あなたが心から仕事を愛し
自分の利害すら忘れて仕事に没頭しているなら
あなたは愛する人生を見つけられるでしょう

たとえ
あなたが愛する人や　愛すべきものを失っても
愛する人とめぐり逢えた喜び　愛すべきものと出会えた喜びは

あなたの
とりとめのない欲望を消し去り
生きている事への　素直な喜びをもたらすものなのです

あなたが
自分の人生を愛すべきものとするには
あなたが自分以外のものを　愛する人になる事です

別離　FOREVER

愛する事は　とても幸せな事かもしれません
愛する事は　とても悲しい事かもしれません

しかし　愛する事を知らぬ人は　もっと不幸な人かもしれません

あなたが愛する人を失った時
それが死別であれ　生き別れであれ
あなたは　悲しみに打ち負かされてしまいそうになるでしょう

しかし　その悲しみこそ
あなたの愛が真実である証ではないでしょうか

あなたの悲しみが深い程　あなたの愛も深く
あたなの悲しみが長い程　あなたの愛も永遠のものである証なのです

だから　あなたが
悲しみに打ちひしがれて倒れそうになったら　こう思えばいいのです

　　　誇りを持とう　真実の愛を持てた私に

そして
愛する人にめぐり逢えた喜びに
真実の愛が　私の人生に見い出せた幸せに感謝しようと

もし　あなたが
愛する人との別離に
それ程の悲しみや　苦しみを感じないとすれば
あなたの人生は　貧しく虚ろでつまらないものと言えるのです

幸せと思った日々でさえ
時を待たず　どんどん色あせたものへと変わっていくでしょう

真実の愛を知らず
真実の喜びも　真実の悲しみも知らぬまま人生を送るより

真実の愛を知り
真実の喜びと　真実の悲しみの中
精一杯生きる人生の　なんと素晴らしい事でしょう

真実の愛を
人生に見い出したあなたは　悲しみの後には
きっと再び　光り輝く喜びを見つけられるに違いありません

存在　GRATITUDE

　　あなたが　この世でひとりぼっちなら
　　あなたは　自分の存在を自覚する事さえ出来ないのです

　　あなたは賢者かも知れません
　　しかし　認めてくれる人もいないのです

　　あなたは正義の人かも知れません
　　しかし　助ける相手もいないのです

　　あなたは美しいかも知れません
　　しかし　他の人の顔を知らないのです

　　あなたは言葉を知っています
　　しかし　話す相手もいないのです

　　あなたは…
　　あなたは…
　　あなたは…

　　あなたは　生きているに違いありません
　　しかし　生きている事さえ自覚するすべもないのです

　　あなたの目に映るものがなければ
　　目をいらないと思うでしょう

　　あなたの話を聞いてくれる人がいなければ
　　口をいらないと思うでしょう

あなたの手を握り返してくれる人がいなければ
手をいらないと思うでしょう

あなたが暗黙の宇宙でひとりぼっちなら
生命さえいらないと思うでしょう

あなたの目を見つめ返してくれる人がいれば
目に感謝出来るのです

あなたの話を聞いてくれる人がいれば
口に感謝出来るのです

あなたの手を握り返してくれる人がいれば
手に感謝出来るのです

あなたが生命あるものに囲まれているなら
あなたは我が生命の大切さに気付くでしょう

目は　あなた以外のものを　見て
口は　あなた以外のものに　話せて
手は　あなた以外のものに　触れられてこそ
生きている思いは　あなたの心に帰って来るのです

あなたは　身体のひとつひとつに感謝し
見えるもの　聞こえるもの　話せるもの　触れられるもの全てに感謝し
言葉ひとつさえ　決して粗末に出来なくなるでしょう

あなたは　目を　口を　手を……　大切にし
身体の全てを　生命ある喜びで満たそうとするでしょう

嘘を言う口を嫌い
優しさのない目を嫌い
思いやりのない手を嫌い
愛を知らぬ我が身を嫌い

あなたは愛する身体のひとつひとつが　愛の仕草に溢れる事を願うでしょう

偶然の幸福　　GENTLY

　　あなたは
　　予期せぬ不幸を
　　運命のいたずらと言って　嘆いてはいないでしょうか

　　そして　あなたは
　　自分の手でつかんだと思う幸福を
　　決して　神のおかげとは言わないでしょう

　神を信じぬあなたは　信じられるのは自分だけだと考え

　　愛すらも信じられないのです
　　そして全てのものが　自分に敵対していると思い込んでしまうのです

　　あなたは
　　幸福は待っていても　得られるものではないと考え
　　全ての幸せは　目的あってのものだと言うのです

　幸福をつかむためには　手段など選ぶ必要はないと言うのです

　　他人にかまっている暇も
　　自分を見つめている暇もないと言うのです

　　あなたにとって
　　優しさは堕落の元凶であり
　　誰かが　幸せになりたいと言ったら

あなたは
勝ち誇ったように　そして厳しく
私と同じ苦労をしなければ駄目だと言うのです

あなたは
手段を選ばず勝ち取った幸福を
いや　時には奪い取ったであろう幸福を
神に感謝しようとは　とても思えないのです

感謝のない幸福が真の幸福でない事を　あなたは知ろうともしないのです

だから　あなたは
常に他人の幸福が気になり　自分の幸福に執着し
決して幸福を人に分け与えようとはしないのです

けれど　あなたには
いつも笑顔で　誰からも好かれる友人がいるのです
彼は　何時も人生を楽しんでいるように見えます

そして何より　彼はあなたより幸福に見えるのです

あなたは
彼の笑顔を憎むでしょう
彼が決して　苦労せずに幸福をつかむ事を憎むでしょう

彼が幸福を人に分け与え　人から愛される姿を憎むでしょう

彼には　幸福を決めつける目的などないのです

彼は　自分を愛するように　人を愛するのです
時には　自分を忘れ人に尽くそうとするのです

しかも　苦労を苦労と思わず
決して笑顔の途切れる事はないのです

彼は
訪れる幸福の　一つ一つに感謝して
自分が幸福に恵まれる資格などないと思い

多くの人に　自分の幸福を分け与えたいと心から思うのです

神は
彼が人を愛するように彼を愛するのです

神は
彼が人の幸福を願うように彼の幸福を願うのです

神は
あなたを映す鏡の中にいるのです

あなたの心が　神に通じ　神の心と一つになった時
あなたの元に　幸福の種が落ちて来るのです

それは偶然の形で
まるであなたが　息をするように

とても自然な姿で　あなたの元にやって来るのです

決して
奇跡のように驚かせたり　奇をてらったりしないもの

あなたにだけそっと分かる
あなたの人生に無理なくおさまるもの

神から送られる幸福に　あなたは心から感謝し
感謝の中に　執着など生まれるはずもなく
あなたはその幸福を　多くの人に分け与える喜びを知る事でしょう

真の幸福は
感謝の心なくしては
決して　得られぬ事をあなたは知るでしょう

マッチの火　SUNLIGHT

　　　　　　　真夜中の広いグランドに灯された
　　　　　　小さなマッチの火は
　　　　　　その深い闇の中で　はっきりと見る事が出来ます

　　　黄昏時　マッチの火は
　　おぼろげにしか　見る事が出来ません
　　まして真昼のグランドで
　　マッチの火に気付く人は
　　ほとんどいない事でしょう

人は悲しみに深く覆われた時　普段気にも留めなかった
　小さな思いやりへの感謝に
　　気付く事が出来るのです
　　　　中途半端な悲しみの時には
　　　　　思いやりの意味さえ　解らない事が多いのです

　　　　だから幸せな人ほど
　　　　　　思いやりを
　　　　　　　　見失いがちなのではないでしょうか

たとえ
　あなたが不幸であろうとも
　　闇の中にいる人の心を知り
　　たとえ何もしてあげられなくとも
　　人を思いやるその心は
　　まるで暗黙の宇宙に輝く
　　太陽の光の如く
　深い悲しみの中にいる人の
愛の光となるのです

CHAPTER 4

自然

GOD

雨　さし出す手

　　映す僕の顔　自然の鏡　手のひらにいっぱい

海　MOTHER

地上には
無数の川があり　どの川の水も絶えず流れています

川が流れるのは
水の行き着く先があるから

海は
川とは比べものにならない程の水量を持ち
しかも
どの川の水をも　無条件で受け入れてくれるのです

無数の川は
互いに合流し
やがて　全ての川は海へ辿り着くのです

海に何色のインクを垂らしても　決してその色に染まる事がないように

川が
どんなに濁流であろうとも
海に帰る時には　透明な海の色となるのです

川にとって　海は
聖なる水であり　無限の愛であり　母なる神　そのものに違いありません

あなたの魂が
人生を送る事が出来るのは
魂の行き着く先があるからに違いありません

あなたの魂も
川の如く　母なる神の元へ流れているのです

それは
あなたとは　比べようもない程の大きな魂であり
しかも
その大なる魂は　あなたを無条件で受け入れてくれるのです

あなたが
恐れず　拒む事さえなければ
あなたを　透明な愛で潔めてくれるのです

海が決して川の流れを拒まぬように　神も決してあなたを拒む事はないのです

海のゆくえ　REINCARNATION

　海は
　　太陽の光を浴び
　　目に見えぬ水蒸気となり　雲となる

　海の水は
　　天の海となり　再び　空にその姿を現わす

　雲は
　　太陽を隠し　人は太陽を見る事は出来ない
　　しかし雲は我が上に　いつも輝く太陽がある事を知っている

　天の海は
　　やがて雨となり　この地へと降ちてくる
　　地上に降ちた雨は　天の海にいた事を忘れていくだろう

　　　雨は　雲であった事を　忘れるだろう
　　　雲は　海であった事を　忘れるだろう
　　　海は　川であった事を　忘れるだろう
　　　川は　雨であった事を　忘れるだろう

　　しかし
　　自然は　それを忘れはしない
　　なぜなら
　　自然は　永遠にそれを見続けているから

　海が
　　穏やかな波の下に　生命を育んでいるように

神は
　穏やかな愛の中に　魂を育んでいる

魂は
　新たなる生命を　待ちきれぬように
　雲となり　雨となり　この世に戻ってくる

太陽は
　日中　強い光の中に　新たなる生命の産声を聞き
　夜　月明りとなり　魂を安らかな眠りへと誘（いざな）う

魂は
　神の元に帰り　前世の記憶を忘れ
　母に抱かれるように神に守られ　新たな生命の旅立ちを待っている

しかし
　魂は　何処へ行くのか知る由もない

　川は　海となる事を知らず
　海は　雲となる事を知らず
　雲は　雨となる事を知らず
　雨は　川となる事を知らず

　しかし
　自然は　それを知っている
　なぜなら
　自然は　永遠にそれを繰り返してきたから

雲は
　風に運ばれていく

風は
　空気の少ない所に流れる空気の事

空は
　神そのもの　愛そのもの

風は
　神の恵みの少なき処
　神の愛の少なき処へと　雲を運ぶ

雲は
　そこで　雨となる

雨は
　やがて　神の愛　新しき生命となる
　花　木　大地　鳥獣……　へとその姿を変える

人は
　流れる川となる
　流れる恵みの水となる

神は
　あなたが　自然の愛そのものとなる事を夢見ている

空(くう) LOVE

空(くう)　一見何もないもののように見える

　　　それは　存在する全てのものが　分け合っている場所なのか
　　　それとも　全てのものに存在する場所を　与えているものなのか

あなたは　明るい光の中
こうして向かい合っている私との間に　何もないという
それは　あなたが空を隔てて
私達が見つめ合っている事を忘れているから

暗がりの中　あなたは私の顔が見えないという
闇が邪魔して　私の顔が見えないという
それは　あなたが
空を隔てて　私達が見つめ合っている事を忘れているから

空(くう)は

　　　闇ではなく　空は透明だから
　　　昼は光を　夜は闇を　映しているだけ

あなたは　空をつかむ事が出来ないから
空を所有する事は　出来ないと思うかもしれない
あなたは　空を飛ぶ事が出来ないから
空を自由にする事は　出来ないと思うかもしれない

しかしあなたは　空がなければ　息をする事が出来ない事を知っている

あなたが　賢者であろうと　愚かであろうと
正義の人であろうと　悪人であろうと　美しくとも　醜くとも

空(くう)は

　　　差別なく　あなたの中に入っていく
　　　そして　誰もが平等に　同じ空を吸っては吐いている

この部屋で
あなたが　私を嫌いであろうとも
あなたは　私の吐いた息を吸い
私は　あなたの吐いた息を吸っている
私とあなたは　互いの息を吸い合っている

あなたが　草原にいれば
あなたの吐く息を　獣や草木が吸い
獣や草木が吐く息を　あなたは吸っている

空(くう)は

　　　全てのものの体内に　平等に流れていく
　　　あなたは　空をつかむ事が出来ない
　　　しかし　いつでも　あなたは
　　　手にするより　もっと深く　空をその体内に吸収している

空(くう)は

　　　晴天の空の青となり　夕焼けの赤となり　七色の虹の色となり
　　　あなたが望む時　いつでも目にする事が出来る

空は　あなたから逃げも隠れもしない
たとえ　あなたがどんな人であろうとも

見上げれば　そこに
誰と　分け隔てすることのない同じ空の姿を　見る事が出来る

空(くう)は

　　　人間にも　獣にも　花にも　草にも……
　　　全てのものに　平等で　自由なのだ

今まで　あなたが　空に感謝した事がないなら
それは　あなたが　空の必要性を考えようとしなかったから

それでも　あなたが　空に感謝できないのは

あなたが自分にだけ　優しくして欲しいと思うから
　　　　　自分だけ　特別扱いにして欲しいと思うから

それは　まるで
赤子が　母親の思いやりに気付かぬようなもの

当然のような顔をして
母親の乳首に吸いつくのと同じようなもの

空(くう)は

　　　あなたの母で
　　　全てのものの母である
　　　まさしく　空は　神の愛の姿そのものなのだ

空 II　*BREATH*

あなたの心が
神すなわち空に　感謝する事が出来なくとも
あなたの体は
空が神の恵みであり　生命の糧である事をよく知っています

その証拠に
あなたが大声で人を罵倒したり　怒鳴ったりしている時
あなたは怒りに全身を震わせて
ものすごい勢いで　空を吐き出すでしょう

あなたの心臓は激しく脈打ち
とぎれとぎれにしか　空を吸う事が出来ません
悲しみや苦しみから　病に倒れるかもしれません

それも　怒り　悲しみ　苦しみで
神である空を　閉ざしているからなのです

あなたが微笑む時
とても軽やかに　とても自然に
あなたは　空を吸っては吐いています

また　あなたが大声で笑う時
あなたはたっぷりと　空を吸っては吐いているのです
あなたの心も体も　幸福な時に違いないでしょう

神は　全てのものに
無条件に与えられる空となり　いつもあなたと共にいるのです

あなたは息をする事で
神を宿し　神を吐き出しているのです

あなたの心が　清らかなものであれば
すなわち　良心と呼べるものであれば
言葉は　神の姿を表わすものとなるのです

神は
人の体に宿り
その人の　言葉や仕草を我が化身として現われるのです

生命の糧となる空
すなわち　神の恵みに対する感謝を持ち
愛を忘れぬ人であれば　誰もが自然に神の化身となり得るのです

聖者　BIG RIVER

雨が
野に降り
種子に入り　花となる

花は
決して動けはしない
しかし見るものの心を和ませてくれる

獣は
食する為だけに　生きるのかもしれない
しかし　我が身もまた
餓食として　他のものの生命の糧となる

人は
恵みの川となる
せせらぎが　結びつき川となる
大きな川は　小さな川をその水量で包み込み
共に一つの河となり　海まで流れて行く

だから
人という字は川という字に似ている
三つの川が結びつき　一つの河となる
人は助け合い　慈しみ合い
心を一つにし　愛を生み　育んでいく

ガンジー　マザー・テレサ
マホメット　イエス　ブッダ……

すべての聖者達は
人を選ばず愛を分かち合い
流れる大河の如く
無数の川を　海なる神の元まで運んでいく

彼らは皆
愛を惜しまず　人を選ばず
ただ　それだけの人と言えるのです

自然　GOD

あなたは木です

森の中に豊かに生い繁る　一本の大きな木なのです
枝には多くの鳥が止まり
あなたの実をついばみ　やがて巣を作り始めます

長い年月が過ぎ　多くの雨風に耐えて
年老いたあなたは　鳥たちのさえずりも　遥か遠くにしか聞く事が出来ません

あなたはやがて朽ち落ち土となるのです

あなたは　鳥のさえずりの代わりに
体の上に様々な動物の足音を聞き
体の中を雨水が流れていくのを感じます

あなたは　土である事を知るのです

あなたは肥え
虫たちは卵を生むのです
卵からかえった幼虫は　あなたを養分として取り入れ地面を這い回るのです

あなたは　虫である事を知るのです

次にあなたは
空から舞い降りてきた鳥についばまれ　鳥の体内に入るのです
あなたは大空を高く飛び
風の音を聞き　今まで見た事のない様々な景色を見るのです
眼下に世界を見下ろして

あなたは鳥である事を知るのです

そして
森の中にそびえる一本の木を見つけ
実をついばみ　やがて巣を作り始めるでしょう

輪廻転生は
時間の中だけに見られるものではありません

この世の同じ空間の中にも
様々な輪廻転生の姿を見る事が出来るのです

全てのものは
全てのものの為に存在し　共に助け合っているのです

全てのものは　一つの心の違った形
心は一つなれど　宿る体によってその役割が違うのです

あなたの体の
手、足、目、口、耳……　がそうであるように

宇宙に存在する　自然全てのものは
一つの心の違う形に　創られたものなのです

そして　その心こそ
神の心そのものであると同時に
神の身体そのものでもあると言えるのです

自然の生命 (かみ いのち) COSMOS

人間は60兆個の細胞により構成されています
そしてその細胞の一つ一つが
自ら生き延びる為　懸命なる努力をしています
互いの細胞の異なる働きが　人間の生命を維持しているのです

人間とは
そのような60兆個の細胞の集合体を　総称したものであると言えるでしょう

あなたを小宇宙とすれば
60兆個の細胞は　全てあなたという宇宙に住み
あなたという小宇宙を構成する　あなたの生命そのものと言えるのです

それと同じように
この雄大なる自然界に生きるもの
あなたを含め他の人間
魚　鳥　獣　草　花　木　地球　月　太陽　そして他の惑星……
存在する全てのものは
自然を構成する自然の生命そのものであり　自然そのものと言えるのです

あなたが天に向かい神に尋ねます
「神よ私は何者でしょう
　神よあなたは私を御存じでしょうか
　神よ私に姿を見せてください」
それはまるで
あなたの中の細胞の一つが　あなたに問いかける姿に似ています
あなたは
自分自身の中の小さな細胞の問いかけに　どう答えるでしょうか

「私が神なら
　君は神である私自身なのだよ
　私を存在させてくれる神の生命そのものなのだ
　君は私と共に生まれ　こうして私と共にいる
　私は君に姿を見せる事は出来ない
　なぜなら
　君は何時も私と一緒にいるのだから
　それでも君が神である私を見たいのなら
　君の見えるもの　君の目に映る全てのものが
　私自身である事を知ればいいのだよ
　存在する全てのものは　私と君とのように一心同体であるのだから」
あなたは　こう答えるしかないのかも知れません

あなたが小宇宙であり
あなたの細胞が　小宇宙を構成するあなたの生命そのものなら
神は大宇宙であり
あなたは　神を構成する神の生命そのものと言えるのです

そして　神とは
遥か宇宙の彼方から　あなたのすぐ足元に及ぶまで
存在する全てのものを言い表わせるもの

すなわち
自然と言えるのです
あなたは自然の生命であり　自然そのものであるのです

CHAPTER 5

ルネッサンスの予感

OLD & NEW

星のない夜

　雲の上には　満天の星空があることを知って欲しい

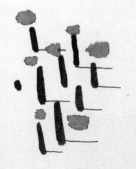

ルネッサンスの予感　OLD & NEW

　　　　地球は

太陽系の中の決められた軌道を動く
惑星の一つであり
人類がそれを知ったのは
長い人類の歴史から見ると　つい最近の事なのです

　　　　　　　　　　　　　　　　　　　　　その昔

　　　　人は地球が球体である事など　想像もつきませんでした
　　　　　　　　　　　　　　　世界は象の背中に乗っている
　　　　　　　　　　　　　　　海の果ては巨大な滝である
　　　　　　　　　　　　そのような事が一般に信じられていました

　　　　そして今

学者たちは　やっと
地球と他の惑星　衛星　彗星などの関係や
宇宙の法則を知り始めたばかりです

　　　　　　　　　　　　　　　　　　　　　現在では

　　　　誰もが地球の存在を知り　宇宙の存在を知っています
　　　　　　　　　　　　地球が太陽の回りを約三百六十五日で公転し
　　　　　　　　　　　約二十四時間で自転している事も知りました

そして月は

地球の回りを約二十九日で公転し　二十九日で自転しています
ですから私達はいつも
月の片側しか見る事が出来ないのです

　　　　　　　　　　　　　　　　　　　潮の満ち引きは

　　　　　　　　　　　月と地球の位置関係によって起こります
　　　　　　　　　　　　月の引力が大きくなる時　潮は満ち
　　　　　　　　　　　　月の引力が小さな時　潮は引くのです

　また火星が地球に接近する時に
地球上に異常気象が発生すると言われています

　　　　　　　　　　　　　　　　　　　このように地球は

　　　　　　　　　　　　　　他の星との位置関係により
　　　　　　　　多くの影響を受けている事が　明らかになってきています

　それと同じように
人間も他の星や月の影響を受けているのです

「地球は青かった」とは

ソ連の宇宙飛行士ガガーリンの有名な言葉ですが
地球の70％を海が覆うように
人体の70％も　水分により構成されているのです

　汗は海水に似た塩辛い味がしますし
海水の比重と人間の体液の比重は
約1.03で共通しているのです

　　　　　　　　　潮の満ち引きが月の引力によって起こるように
　　　　　人の生まれる時は満ち潮の時が多く死ぬ時は引潮の時が多いのです

　また統計学によると
満月の夜の犯罪率は　極端に多くなると言われています

　サキの有名な小説
『狼男』が世界的ベストセラーになったのも
人は無意識に
満月の持つ奇妙な力に
気付いていた為かも知れません

　　　　　　　　　　　　　　　女性の生理の周期も
　　　　　　　　　　　　　　月の自転・公転と同じく
　　　　　　　　　　　　約二十九日ごとにやって来ます

月や他の星が人間におよぼす影響は
まだまだあるのかも知れません

　　　　　　　　　　西洋の占星術は
　　　　　　　　　星の位置関係を使った統計学と言えますが

　　　　　　　　それは科学がまだ未熟な時代に

　　　　　　　　　　多くの人の運命を観察する事で
　　　　　　　　　月や星の運行や位置と人間との関係に
　　　　　　　何らかの原因を見い出した結果生まれたものと言えるでしょう

　　地球の生命を支えていくのに

大切なものに重力があります
月に引力があり地球にも引力があり
全ての星々が影響し合うのは　皆　重力があるからと言えるでしょう

　　　　　　　　　　　　　　　　重力は

　　　　　　　　　　目に見えず　触れる事も出来ません
　　　　　　　　　　　　けれどもその存在や影響力は
　　　　　　　　　　　　様々な形で確認されているのです

そして星々の持つ重力により

宇宙の法則が成り立っているように
魂は人間の運命を握る重力と言えるのかも知れません

　　　　　　　　　　　　　　魂は重力と同じように

　　　　　　　　　　　　　　　見る事も触れる事も出来ません
　　　　　　　しかし　人の運命と深く関わっているのかも知れません

　　　重力が引力となり

全ての星々が結びついて銀河となり
銀河が結びついて宇宙となるように

　　　　　　　　　　　　　　魂も目に見えぬその力により
　　　　　　　　　　　　全ての生命とつながっているのかも知れません

あなたが東と

信じつづけている方角は　宇宙の一点から見れば
西かも知れないし　南かも知れない
なぜなら　地球は絶えず自転と公転を繰り返しているから

　　　　　　　　　　　　　　　あなたが学んだ事も

　　　　　　　　信じて疑わぬ事も　宇宙の真理の中では
　　　　　　　　　ほんのちっぽけなものかも知れない

　　天文学者が

宇宙の謎を解き明かすように
私達も　魂の法則を探り出す必要があるのかも知れません

　　　　　　　　　　　　　　　　　　星の運命が

　　　　　　　銀河ひいては　宇宙全体に委ねられているように
　　　　　人の運命も　自然の摂理によるものかも知れないからです

魂と肉体　RULE

現世における　魂と肉体の関係は
人と家の関係に置き換えてみる事が出来ます

魂を　あなたに
肉体を　あなたの住む家と考えてください

あなたが自分の家に住んでいるように
あなたの魂は　あなたの肉体に宿っているのです

家が
あなたの経済的事情　家庭的　社会的条件などにより
その大きさ　格式　場所などが限定されるように

あなたの肉体もまた
あなたの魂の様々の条件　制約により
その生まれ　容姿　能力などが選ばれているのです

あなたが様々の事情　制約から
理想とする家に住むのが容易でないように

あなたの魂もまた
様々の制約から　理想とする肉体に宿る事はとても難しい事なのです

それは　あなた自身が
自分の家柄　本籍地　容姿　才能などを　選択する事なく
この世に生まれてきた事実からも　理解出来るでしょう

魂が肉体に宿る時　すなわち　出生の産声を上げる時
「魂の制約」により　あなたは宿るべき肉体を与えられているのです

この魂の制約を　仏教ではカルマとか因縁と言うのでしょう

けれども　あなたが
今の自分の生い立ち　容姿　性格　才能　健康など

あらゆる事に満足できず
悲しみや苦しみに打ちひしがれていても　決して諦める事はありません

あなたの心が変化する事により
あなたは自由自在に　変化する事が出来るのです

たとえば
人生に喜びを感じられず

家に帰っても
その悲しみに打ちひしがれるばかりの人は

家を掃除する気力も　湧かないばかりか
家の修繕もせずに　放っておく事でしょう

そのような家主の住む家は　どんどん傷みが激しくなり
何十年も経ったように荒れ果て　ボロボロになっていくのです

肉体も家のように
そこに宿るあなたの心が　喜びを見い出せず
悲しみ苦しみを繰り返すばかりの人であるなら

あなたの肉体は益々衰え　病や災いに犯されていくでしょう

精神的なイライラや緊張状態が　血液の流れを不規則にして
心筋梗塞の発作が引き起こされるように

心の持ち方が
病気を引き起こす事も　しばしばあるのです

魂の制約により幸福に恵まれ　非情に健康な肉体を持ったとしても
あなたの心が　平安を見い出せるものでなければ
あなたの肉体は　病弱なものに変わってしまうのです

不正　虚偽　まやかしを働く人の顔
憎しみ　妬み　怒りに満ちた人の顔
絶望　不安　悲しみに捕われている人の顔は
どれも美しくないものばかりです

それと同じように　あなたが
どんなに美しい容姿に生まれたとしても
あなたの心がけが悪ければ　醜い姿に変わってしまうのです

住む人が　暗く闇のようなものなら
家は　加速的に朽ち果てていくように

あなたも　心を闇に置くのなら
肉体もまた　時を待たずに滅んでいくのです

あなたが　自分の心を不満としておく事は
あなたの肉体を　粗末にしているのと同じ事なのです

それと反対に
人生に満足し　仕事にも喜びを見い出し
人間関係においても　喜びを感じている人の家は
とても気持ちの良いものです

天気の良い日には　家の窓は大きく開かれ
陽の光と新鮮な空気が　家中を満たしている事でしょう

そのような家は　古さを感じさせないばかりか
年月を経てきたものだけが持つ味わいや
住み心地の良さを感じさせる　素敵な家となっていく事でしょう

あなたの魂が
愛　幸福　希望　喜び　そして平安に満ちているのなら
あなたの肉体もまた
病や災いから解き放たれ　美しく光り輝く事になるのです

もしあなたが

自分の生い立ちを卑下していようとも
病弱の肉体に悩んでいようとも
容姿に自信がなくとも
自分に才能を感じられなくとも

あなたの心が　喜びで満たされ
ありのままの自分の姿に　感謝する事が出来れば
あなたは　美しく輝き始めるのです

人は誰しも

生まれながらに美しい容姿を持ち
立派で裕福や家柄に育ち
豊かな才能と強い肉体を　持ちたいと思うものです

不幸にも
全てがあなたの理想と違っていても
あなたの心が　ありのままの自分の姿を愛し慈しみ
喜びの心を持つ事が出来れば　あなたの人生は光り輝くのです

逆に幸運にも
恵まれた運命の第一歩を得られても
心のあり方が正しくなければ　あなたの人生は闇と化すのです

魂の制約は
神が創ったものかも知れません

しかし　心は
あなた自身のものなのです
あなたが何を思おうと　あなたが何を感じようと

神は　あなたの心まで　制約しようとはしていないのです

あなたの心は

あなた自身が自由に羽ばたく事の出来る　無限の空と言えるのですから

記憶　POSSESSION

この世に授かった生命とは
現世の記憶　と言い換える事が出来ます

この世で生命を失くすとは
多くの場合　現世での記憶を失くすという事なのです

あなたは知り合った全ての人々
親　子供　夫　妻　恋人　友人……

体験した全ての事
喜び　悲しみ　希望　安らぎ　驚き……

それら　一切の記憶を失くすのです

愛した事も　憎んだ事も　笑った事も　泣いた事も
その全てが　あなたから消えていき
あなたは自分の顔ばかりか　名前さえ忘れていくのです
安らかな眠りとは　そういう事なのではないでしょうか

すでに肉体を失くしたあなたが
現世の記憶に縛られる事は
五体を縛られ　動かぬ体で野に放り出されるように
どうしようもなく苦しい事に　違いないからです

肉体を失くした後
記憶だけが　そのまま存在するのなら
それは未来永劫にわたる苦しみを　生む事になるのです

肉体を持たぬ為
叶えられぬ欲望は一層つのり
他の生命ある者の体を借りても
その思いを　遂げようとするかも知れません

泣きたくても泣ける肉体を持たず　怒りたくても怒れる肉体を持たず
死にたくても死ねる肉体を持たず　その永遠の苦しみから解放される為
生命ある者の中に　我が欲望を宿らそうとするのです

現世で生命を終える時
無に帰れてこそ　幸せであると知るべきなのです

あなたが　現世での記憶を失くしてこそ
新しい輪廻転生の中で
次なる生命を持つ喜びを　経験する事が出来るのです

あなたは　与えられた寿命を生き
人生に喜びを見い出せるよう
日々の生活の中で　愛と努力を惜しまぬ事が大切なのではないでしょうか

憑依　QUARK

　　人間の感覚とは　大脳の神経細胞の働きであると言えます
　　見えるという事は　大脳の視覚中枢を作っている細胞が
　　目から入った情報の分析を　行なっている結果と言えるのです

　　しかも　脳細胞はあなたの意識するものだけでなく
　　あなたの意識せぬものも　瞬時に情報分析するといった素晴らしいものなのです

　　例えば　あなたがこうして私と話をしている
　　当然あなたは私の顔しか　意識していないにも関わらず
　　私の服の色も　後ろにあるカーテンの色や　本棚に並ぶ様々な本や
　　テーブルの上のコーヒーカップまで　あなたには見えています

　　それは　あなたの脳細胞はあなたの意識に関わらず
　　あなたの視野に映る全てのものの情報を
　　瞬時にして　分析処理しているという事です

　　人間の感覚は　あなたが意識しようとしまいと
　　細胞の働きによって　引き起こされているという事です
　　言い換えると　あなたの思考と行動は　細胞によって決定されているのです

　　同じ原因から生じる　思いや感情が人によって違うのは
　　各個人の持つ細胞の働きが異なる為であり　見えるという事実も
　　各個人の脳細胞の分析能力の大小　または　正常異常により
　　違った分析結果を　もたらすものとなるのです

　　コロンブスが初めて　アメリカ大陸を発見した時
　　アメリカインディアンには　コロンブスの船が見えなかったという説があります

それは当時のインディアンが　船というものを全く理解出来なかった為に
視野にある船の情報処理を脳細胞が
分析出来なかったからと　言えるのかも知れません

また　精神に異常をきたしている人や　薬物を乱用している者は
視野にないもの　すなわち幻覚を見ますが
これは異常を起した脳細胞による　異常な分析によるものと言えるでしょう

時として　異常な精神変化を
憑依という言葉に　置き換えられる事がありますが
憑依された人とは　脳細胞に異常をきたしている人だけを言うのでしょうか
しかし　憑依の原因が霊体によるものなら
霊体も　記憶　思考エネルギーを持つ何らかの物質であるに違いありません

人体の細胞は　原子によって構成されています
しかもその原子は固い粒ではなく　原子核と電子から構成され
さらに原子核は　素粒子という小さな物質の集まりであるところまで
現代の科学は突き止めています

このように見ると　細胞は素粒子の集合体であり
人間は　その膨大な数の素粒子の働きによって生命を維持し
記憶　思考　を持ち合わせていると言えます

人間の記憶　思考　が大脳の原子を構成する素粒子の働きによるものならば
素粒子の一つ一つが　記憶　思考　を持ち合わせていると言えます

あなたの大脳素粒子をいくつか取り出し　私の大脳に組み入れれば
私はその素粒子の持つ　記憶　思考　を得る事になり
あなたは　それを失くすという事になります

その素粒子が悲しみの感情を持つものなら
私は突然泣き出すかも知れません

強烈なシーンを記憶しているものなら
視野にないものが見えたりする事もあり得るでしょう

人体は一見　隙間のないもののように見えますが
素粒子のレベルで眺めると　隙間だらけなのです
だから素粒子はいとも簡単に　人体を出たり入ったり出来るものかも知れません

仮に　記憶　思考　を持つ素粒子が人体の細胞原子のみならず
空気を構成している原子や分子と共に
空間に存在しているという事にでもなれば
いつ　人体の中に飛び込んでくるかも知れません

人体は膨大な数の素粒子
そして　それらが集まって出来た原子が
調和とバランスを保って　成り立っているものなのですから
ここに別の素粒子が入り込んでくると
バランスを保っていた人体の細胞の働きが　狂い始めるのです
それは　神経機能と生命機能に異変をもたらす事となるのです

突如として　見えるはずのないものが見えたり
聞こえるはずのないものが聞こえたり
経験した事のない記憶が湧き出たり　意味不明な感情に襲われたり
原因不明の体調不全や　病気を引き起こしたりする事もある得るでしょう

霊体が　記憶　思考　を持つ見えぬ物質であり
素粒子こそが　その見えぬ物質の正体であるなら
霊体を　科学的　生物学的に分析する事は可能だと言えるでしょう

憑依とは　その素粒子によって引き起こされる
精神的　肉体的　悪影響を言うのかも知れません

原因不明の過失　原因不明の病気
例えば　精神障害のなかった健全な父親が
何の原因もなく我が子を殺害したり
突如として起こる精神分裂などには
素粒子による悪影響が　原因しているケースがあるのかも知れません

最近の医学は　病気の原因究明を細胞レベルから
さらに　ミクロのレベルで研究していく方向にあります

生命活動は　突き詰めて言うなら
原子や分子　さらには素粒子の働きによって行なわれるものです
医学の進歩は　素粒子の新たなる影響の発見によっては
宗教との接点がもたらされる可能性が　充分にあると考えられるでしょう

宇宙と時間 0×60=60

宇宙は絶えず膨張しています
川が　その川幅を増していくのは
絶えず新しい流れを　受け入れているから

宇宙も川と同じように　新しい何かを受け入れているのかもしれません

人の成長の瞬間を　見る事が出来ないように
宇宙もまた　その膨張の瞬間を見る事は出来ないのかもしれません

人は常に成長を結果としてしか　見る事が出来ない
宇宙も常に膨張を結果としてしか　見る事が出来ないのかもしれません

人が太っていくのは　食物を食べるから
宇宙もまた　膨張するのは何かのエネルギーを取り入れているから

宇宙が摂取するエネルギーの　正体を探るため
私達は時間を止め　膨張の瞬間と対面する必要があると言えるでしょう

当然その瞬間　宇宙の膨張は止まり
太陽も地球も他の銀河の星々も　動きを止めてしまいます

この瞬間すなわち　宇宙の膨張する瞬間に宇宙は膨張していない

しかし宇宙は　この瞬間にこそ
膨張する為に必要なエネルギーを　取り入れているのです
それはまさしく　瞬間という時間そのものではないでしょうか

瞬間を突き詰めていくと
静止の状態にまで行き着く事になります

瞬間とは静止している状態
すなわち　時間が止まっている状態

時間とは静止が積み重なって　生まれるもの
それはまるで　無から有が生まれるようなもの
0秒が積み重なり　時の数字が生まれていく

0×60=0　でなく60という時を刻む

ブラックホールでは
0×60=－60にも　－600にも変化する
時間は存在するものの中で　自由自在に変化していくのかも知れません

物理学でも20世紀になって
時間もエネルギーを持つ事が発見されました
有名なのはアインシュタインの相対性理論です

時間とは何でしょうか
人が時間を知るのは　光と影があるから

写真の中のものが動かないのは　光と影が焼き付けてあるから
瞬間の光と影を焼き付けた写真の中には　瞬間という時が入っている

影は光によって生まれ
光は影を持つ

瞬間とは光と影が重なる時
時間の流れとは
光と影が重なり合い　積み重なったもの

時間とは
存在した全てのもの　存在する全てのもの　存在しようとする全てのものを
積み重ねた無限なるエネルギーと言えるのです

この無限なる時間のエネルギーを得て
『宇宙』という存在は膨張を続けているのかもしれません

宇宙を創ったといわれる
ビッグバンも

存在した全てのものと
存在する全てのものと
これから　存在しようとする全てのものの

無限なるエネルギーによる　作用なのかもしれません

CHAPTER 6

小さな恐竜
HUMAN BEINGS

風が時を運び、時が季節に変わる

　　　　僕はもう春にいない

言葉　*ISOLATION*

　右脳に浮かんだイマジネーションが
　左脳で言葉に変わる時
　私は心の全てを　伝えられないもどかしさを感じる
　心は言葉という　ふるいにかけられ表現される
　心を言葉にすると　完全な形で伝える事は出来ない

　どんなに愛していようとも
　言葉にすると　とても愛してる　としかならないように
　しかし　私は知っている
　自分の思いを……　どれ程愛しているか………

　だけど　愛は言葉というふるいにかけられ　選択されてしまう
　ふるいからもれた愛を　伝えるすべはない

　人類は　言葉を持った時から
　文明と引き替えに　大切な何かを失くし始めたのかもしれない

動物は　言葉を持たずとも解り合える
魚も　鳥も　獣も　群れを成して生きていく

しかも　同じ生物種とのコミュニケーションのみに留まらず
魚や　鳥や　獣が　天災から事前に逃避出来るように
この自然(かみ)の意識の何かと
どこかで通じ合っているのかもしれない

なのに　人間は
言葉を持つ者としか　充分なコミュニケーションが出来ないと
信じ始めたのかもしれない

人は無意識にも　心と言葉の隙間に吹く風の儚(はかな)さを知り
芸術を生み出したのかもしれない

芸術は　言葉に出来ぬ心を　表現したもの
人は　音楽や　絵で　共通の心を分かち合える気がする
しかし　それは　自然(かみ)の意識とは別のもの

私達人類が　言葉と引き替えに失くしてきた心と
通じ合える何かが　この自然界には存在し
私達人類だけが
その何かを見失い　自然全てのものと　孤立しているのかもしれない

超能力　MELODY

鳥や魚は　地震や火山爆発の前その場所から離れ
安全な所へ逃避する事が出来る

野生の鳥は　空を自由に飛び生きていく
かごの鳥は　とりかごから放すと死んでいく

昔　人は
風の音を枕に大地に寝そべり　岩に腰を下ろし
夕陽を見ていた

今　土の匂いを避け
コンクリートの上に暮らし　プラスチックの椅子に腰掛け
TVを見ている

自然との対話を避け　科学を追い
直感を信じず　理論を重んじる
内なる声を聞かぬ耳は
もはや　51字で綴られる言葉しか聞こえず
自然(かみ)の声を聞く事はない

人もかつて　自然(かみ)の子そのものだった

なのに　人だけが本来の姿
それは自然(かみ)から創造された姿から　良くも悪くも大きく変化した
人の進歩を科学の進歩と　結びつけるのは決して間違いとは言えないだろう

しかしその結果　人は本来の能力を失ってきた
それは些細な事で見れば
靴がなければ　歩けない事かもしれない
病に薬がなければ　不安でならない事かもしれない
人は常に科学から生み出されたものに　頼らなければならなくなった

それでも人は
かごの鳥のように飛び立つ事を忘れ　満足しきっているかのように見える

とりかごは科学の砦であり
人は理論で　立証出来ぬ事に強い恐怖を持つようになる
恐怖は人をさらに科学へと結びつける

しかし　それはとりかごを頑丈にするばかりで
外の世界への恐怖をますます募らせる事となる

自然(かみ)とのバリケードを　張り巡らせる事ばかりに夢中になり
無限の空を　羽ばたく夢を見る事さえ忘れてしまう

科学は自然現象を解明する事から　生まれたものなのに
自然(かみ)から人間に与えられた自由なる力を　奪い取ろうとしている

かごの鳥も自然に育まれた自然(かみ)の旋律の一つだった
人も　自然に育まれ自然(かみ)のメロディーを奏でていた
なのに人は　自然の声に耳を傾ける事はなく
内なる自然(かみ)のメロディーを口ずさむ事もない

小さな恐竜　HUMAN BEINGS

今から 6550 万年前
地球上の支配者であった　恐竜が滅んだ原因について
様々な議論が繰り返されてきましたが
最近になって　巨大隕石の地球への落下　という説が
最も有力なものとして捉えられています

ある学者によると　直径約 10 キロメートルもの隕石が地球に落下し
一瞬のうちに　恐竜ばかりか
白亜紀に生存していたほとんどの生物を　絶滅に追いやったというのです

こういった生物の集団絶滅は　恐竜だけでなく
過去　地球上に出現した数々の生物にも見られる事が
化石の研究からも明らかにされています

生物の集団絶滅は　約 6 億 7 千万年前の
三葉虫から　アンモナイト　フズリナ　など大小合わせて 18 回
それも約 2600 万年ごと　定期的に繰り返されているのです

そういった事から科学者の中には
宇宙にその原因を探る者も数多く現われています
非常に長い周期で　地球にやって来る彗星の嵐を
その原因とするものや
地球の軌道と交差する　直径約 5 キロメートル以上の小惑星を
その原因とするものなど様々です

動物は植物の環境の中で　その生命を維持しています
植物は地質と大気により生まれ育ちます　死した惑星から種は育ちません

すなわち　植物の存在は
水と同様に地球が　生命を持つ惑星である事の基本的証拠と言えるのです

白亜紀の終わり頃　地球上の支配者であった恐竜は
巨大化しながらも　恐ろしいまでの増殖を繰り返し
その食欲は地球上の全ての植物を
食い尽くす恐れが充分あったと言えるのです

それはいずれ　他の生物が生まれ育たぬ事を意味し
ひいては地球自身が
恐竜と共倒れになる可能性すら　充分にあったと言えるのです

丁度それが　6550万年前
巨大隕石の落下により　幕を下ろした理由(わけ)ですが……

これが　宇宙の偶然の出来事によるものか　何かの意志によるものかと
考えるのは　非情に興味深いものです

なぜなら　それ以来地球上には恐竜は出現せず
隕石の落下は　地球の体質と環境を変え　植物はその種を変え
動物はその生態を恐竜と比べ
より小型の哺乳類へと変化させてきたからです

自然の意志によるものか　どうかはともかく
隕石の落下による　地球の体質と環境の急変化が
人類を創造した事に変わりはありません

まさしく人類は　自然の選択により出現したと言えるのです
そして人類が誕生して　約300万年の間
この小さな哺乳類は　自然との調和を図るように生存してきたのです

恐竜の食欲に　おびえる事のない地球は
かつてない程の穏やかな気候を　生物にもたらしてきたのです

1954年ローマで開かれた　第一回世界人口会議で
当時25億であった世界人口は
1980年には35億になるだろうと
予測されましたが　実際には44億に達してしまいました

20世紀初め10億だった世界人口は
21世紀中には100億にもなるだろうと言われています

人類は自然採取により　食糧を得る事から
食糧を　栽培　生産　保存　する事を覚えました
農業革命さらには産業革命により　人口は驚く程急増しているのです

人類は　自然を人類の繁栄の為だけに　作り変えようとしています
その結果　地球上から多数の生物が絶滅し
人類だけが　恐ろしいまでに増加し続けているのです

今　人類は白亜紀の終わり頃　繁殖し続ける恐竜が生き延びる為
他の多くの生物を　その餌食としていた姿にひどく似かよっています

かつて恐竜が　地球という巨大な生命体を蝕む　ガン細胞であったように
人類もその巨大な人口増加により　まるで小さな恐竜の如く
地球のガン細胞と　成りつつあるのかもしれません

6500万年前　地球は　自らの生命を守る為
「巨大隕石の落下による大手術」により
地球上の支配者を　恐竜から哺乳類へと変化させ
私達人類にその夢を託したのかもしれません

人類は恐竜と比べようもない程
食糧供給量が小さく　優れた頭脳を持つ哺乳類であったのです

地球は本来　微惑星が衝突し合って創られた生命を持つ　巨大な惑星なのです
その生命の本源は　宇宙にあると考えれば
「巨大隕石による大手術」も納得のいくところではないでしょうか

人類の歴史において　科学の進歩は常に自然との対決のようでしたが
今　私達は人類の生命を生み育んでくれる
この宇宙を含む自然全てに対して　感謝と思いやりを忘れず
自然との調和を図っていく　必要があるのではないでしょうか

科学や物理などにおける学問においても　クールな視点からだけではなく
愛ある視点で取り組む姿勢が　強く望まれるのではないかと思われます

1972年8月　アメリカ・ワイオミング州に住む
ジェームス・ベーカーが観光旅行中に撮影していた8mmカメラの中に
地球の大気圏をかすめて飛び去った
重さ約1000トン　直径約5キロメートル以上もの
巨大な隕石が偶然撮られていました

アメリカ政府がその事実を発表したのは　ベーカーよりかなり後の事でした
この巨大隕石が地球に衝突していたら
私達人類は彗星の嵐も　交差する小惑星も待たずして絶滅していた事でしょう

そして　地球の体質と環境は急変化し
人類にとって替わる新しい種が　生まれ育まれていくでしょう
それはまるで　人類の犯した過ちを
二度と繰り返さないよう願う　自然(かみ)の意志によるものかもしれません

タイムマシン　NO FUTURE

　　　1988年

タイムマシンが理論上実現可能であるという
論文がアメリカで発表され話題を呼びました

　　　　　　　　　　　　　　タイムマシンという
　　　　　　　　　　　　人類の夢の実現性について
　　　　　　　　語れる事は非常に楽しみな事に違いありません

　　　しかし

視点を変えれば　ここにもう一つの
確かな真実を　知る事が出来るのです

　　　　　　　　　　　　　　　　　　確かな真実とは
　　　　　　　　　今　タイムマシンが存在していないという事実です

　　　つまり　学説通り

人類が将来　タイムマシンを手にする事が可能なら
現在　過去において　タイムマシンが飛来してきている
確かな既成事実があるはずです

しかし　私達は

小説や映画の中でしか　タイムマシンに
関する情報を　見たり聞いたりする事が出来ないのです

　　　　　　　　　　　　　　　　　　　　その現実は

　　　　　　　　人類はタイムマシンを　永遠に手に入れられないという
　　　　　　　　　　　結論に結びつけてしまうのではないでしょうか

　学者は往々にして

紙面上の計算によってのみ物事を作り出しますが
顔を上げれば　現実はすでにその答えを出している
という事は決して少なくないのです

　　　　　　　　　　　　　　　　　　　　　私達はここに
　　　　　　　　　科学の盲点を垣間見る事が出来るのではないでしょうか

　それを象徴的に表わしているのが
今度のタイムマシンの論文といえるのかもしれません

コペルニクスが
地動説を公表したのは1543年の事です

　　　　　　　　　　　　　　　それまで　人類は

　　　　　　　　　　地球が動いている現実の中にいても
　　　　　　　　　　　　　天動説を信じ続けてきたのです

　　　人類の知性は

不変の現実に対面しても
素直に真実を受け入れる事が出来ないのかもしれません

　　　　　　　　　　　　　　　　　　タイムマシンが

　　　　　存在し得ないという事実から　貴重な仮説を得られる事が解ります

　　　それは　タイムマシンが

理論上　可能なものであっても　不可能なものであっても
私達人類は　タイムマシンを　永遠に手中にする事はないという事です

つまり　私達人類は

タイムマシンを創れる科学の時代まで
生き延びる事が出来ない　という真実です

　　　　　　　　　　　　　ある学者が　タイムマシンは
　　　　　　　　　100年後には実現するという確信を持つなら

　　　人類は
100年以内に死滅してしまうという事です

　　　　　　　　　　　　それが　500年後　1000年後であっても

　　　人類は
その時まで生き延びていないという事になるのです

　　　　　　　　　　　　　　　　　　これは

　　　　　　　　　　　タイムマシンを基準として
　　　得られる　人類の寿命といえるのではないでしょうか

タイムマシンが

実現性を持ち始める程　人類の歴史は
終焉に近づいているといえるのです

　　　　　　　　　　　　　　アインシュタインは

　　　　相対性理論を発表し　タイムマシンの実現性について
　　　　　　確かな可能性を見い出したのかもしれませんが

　それと同時に　今

タイムマシンが存在していない矛盾に
人類の終焉が近い事を知ったのかもしれません

　　　　　　　　　　　　　　世界で唯ひとりでも

　　　人類がタイムマシンを操っている場面に　遭遇する事があるなら
　　　人類は永遠の未来を　手に入れている証拠となるのですが…………

UFOを

タイムマシンと仮定するなら
スピルバーグの「E.T.」に描かれているような宇宙人は

　　　　　　　　　　　　　　　　　　　　　遠い未来

　　　　人類滅亡後　地球のリーダーとなる新しい生物なのかもしれません

　　シンプルな身なりと

小さい肉体に　巨大な頭脳を持つその生物は
一見して　人類より遥かに
肉欲の少ない生物のように　想像する事が出来ます

　　　　　　　　　　　　　　　　　　　人類滅亡後の

　　　　　　地球のリーダーとして　自然との調和を図るには
　　　　ふさわしい資質をもつ　新しい生物の姿なのかもしれません

タンポポ　SPRING

春、丘の上にタンポポの花が咲くでしょ。
一年が 365 日あって、タンポポの咲いている、あの時間って一ヶ月位かな
タンポポが、僕だとするとタンポポのしおれていく時が、僕の寿命
僕は暑い夏の日差しも、秋のそよ風も、冬の雪も、知らない
ただ、春になって咲く花が、僕なんです。
地球には必ず、四季があって 365 日たてば、同じ季節がやってきます。
その時ね、僕の咲いていた同じ丘の上に
僕と違うタンポポの花が咲くんです。
彼は、ちょうど一年前に、僕が咲いていた事なんて知らないんです。
初めて、丘の上に顔を出して、若草の匂いなんか嗅いだりして
自分が、いつしおれていくなんて考えもしないし
地球に四季があって、今が春だって事もなんにも知らないんです。
僕が春のおだやかな、天気の下で生きてたみたいに
彼も雪がとけ、暖かくなった土の上で咲いた後
むせかえるような暑さの前には、もう、消えているんでしょうね。

CHAPTER 7

光のごとく
MISTY

若草の匂い　流れる雲

　　風の下　遠くから僕を呼ぶ友の声

光のごとく MISTY

真昼の太陽
まぶしい祝福の光
全てのものを照らします
その目もくらむ明るさの中
水面には
太陽の姿は見い出せず
光の粒がキラキラと輝いて見えるのです
そして水面は
光に満ち溢れた辺りの風景を
美しく鮮やかに映し出すのです
それは
あなたが喜びの時
見るもの全てが美しく輝いて見える時
あなたが神の必要を感じない程幸福な時
それでも
神はあなたのそばにいて
あなたを祝福してくれているのです

夜の月
ほのかな光
全てのものの輪郭を
ぼんやりと照らします
おだやかな光は
暗いまわりの風景の中
鏡に映るが如く
きわだって水面に輝いて見えるのです
それは
あなたが苦しみを感じる時
悲しみで目がかすみ
目の前のものですらよく見る事が出来ない時
今すぐにでも神の助けが必要な時
あなたが求めさえすれば
神はいつまでも見続ける事の出来る
やさしい月の光となって
あなたを見守っているのです

一瞬の彼方　　*SHADOW*

　　あなたは　この一瞬の出来事が
　　人生の全てのように思い
　　この一瞬の彼方を　心に思い描く事はない

　　だから
　　あなたは今の私を見て
　　私がたとえ
　　善であろうと　悪であろうと　賢者であろうと　愚かであろうと
　　私の事を決め付けてしまう

　　あなたの決め付けた私が　一瞬のものでも
　　あなたにとっては　永遠のものとなり
　　私が変わろうが　変わるまいが
　　あなたは私の一瞬の影を　永遠に心に塗り付ける

　　あなたは　私の消えた影を永遠に見続ける
　　それは　あなた自身にも言える事

　　あなたが今　苦しみの中にいても
　　それは束の間の　あなたの影にすぎないのかもしれない
　　それをあなたは　永遠のものと思う
　　だからあなたは永遠に　救いがないと思うのかもしれない
　　だからあなたは　死にたいとすら思うのかもしれない

一瞬のあなたの影が　影のない未来を闇で覆う
あなたの影は　あなたが動くと変化する
あなたが　動かなくとも変化する

あなたの生き方が影を変え
時の流れが影を消す

一瞬の影は　あなたから生まれ
自然(かみ)の中に　解き放される

あなたの過去は　すでに
あなたの手を離れ　自然(かみ)の手の中に委ねられる

しかし　あなたは
一瞬の影を引きずるように生きている

なぜなら
あなたは　この一瞬が
あなた自身の過去から　運ばれてきた事を知っているから
そして　この一瞬は
未来に通じる　大切なものである事を知っているから

一瞬を　生きる事
それは　執着をなくし　歩み続ける事なのだ

夢　　STORY

　　あなたは
　　自分のみる夢の行方を　知っているでしょうか

　　夢はあなたが　創り出すものであるはずなのに
　　夢の作家は　あなた自身であるはずなのに

　　あなたは　ストーリーを知らない主人公のように
　　夢の中で　一喜一憂するのです

　　現実のあなたも夢の中のあなたと　同じではないでしょうか

　　あなたの人生は
　　あなた自身が　創り出すものであるはずなのに
　　人生のストーリーは　あなた自身が描けるはずなのに

　　あなたは　ストーリーをつかめぬ主人公のように
　　現実の中で　一喜一憂しているのではないでしょうか

　　あなたの夢が
　　あなたの記憶から生まれるように

結果には必ず原因が存在し
結果は次なる原因となるのです

あなたの現在は　あなたの過去と未来の間で
一本の糸のように　結びつき

現在のあなたは　過去のあなたの結果であり
未来のあなたは　現在のあなたの延長なのです

現在のあなたを知りたければ
過去のあなたを思い浮かべて見るのです

未来のあなたを知りたければ
現在のあなたを見つめてみれば良いのです

こうしてあなたは
ストーリーをつかめぬ　夢の中の主人公のように
現実の中で　一喜一憂する事はなくなり

実り豊かな人生を送る事の出来る　自らの人生の作家と成り得るのです

ぶどうの房　*A PIECE OF HEART*

心は
ぶどうの房のように
あなたという生命の枝に咲くぶどうの実の味がする

心は
ひとつでなく
いくつもの思いが集まったもの

枝が
成長するにつれぶどうの実もふえていく

子供の頃
あなたの房には　実がひとつしかなく
あなたの心が手に取るようにわかった

今
あなたの房には
色々な味のするぶどうの実がなっている

あなたの実を食べて
美味しいという人もまずいという人もいるだろう

あなた自身
どれが自分のぶどうの実の味かわかりはしない

だけど
あなたは美味しいと言われるぶどうの実を大切にする

　　　　　幼い頃のあなたは
　　　　まだ　実のならないぶどうの房

　　　　　　人は誰も
　　　　あなたの実を　食べようとしない

　　　　　　　しかし
　　　あなたが　豊かで美味しいぶどうの房になる事を願っている

　　　　　少年のあなたは
　　　　　まだ　蒼いぶどうの房
　　たとえ　誰かが食べて苦くても　決してあなたの責任にはしない

　　　　　青年のあなたは
　　　　甘ずっぱいぶどうの房

　　　　　　　人は
　　ひとつぶ　味見してはもう少し熟れるのを待っている

　　　　　大人のあなたは
　　　　　熟れたぶどうの房

　　　　　　　人は
　　　安心してあなたを口いっぱい　ほおばる
　中に　まずいぶどうの実があればあなたの責任にしたりする

　　　　　　　季節が
　何度も過ぎあなたは季節の数だけぶどうの実を咲かしてきた

季節が流れ
年老いたあなたの枝に
ぶどうの実は咲かなくなり　人は誰もあなたのそばに集まらなくなった

あなたは
ひとりぼっちで
昔　豊かに咲いたぶどうの実の事を思い出す

今
あなたにとっては
全ての実がどれも美味しく感じられる

冬が来て
あなたは　枯れ　朽ち
土となり記憶さえもなくしてしまう

何度目かの夏

昔
あなたのいた場所に
あなた木から
こぼれ落ちたぶどうの種が　いつの間にか大きなぶどうの木に育ち

枝には
豊かなぶどうの実が　いっぱい　咲いていた

The Dreams of God

CHAPTER 1

The Moon
CONSCIENCE

Sunlight shines from afar

I have a feeling I'm going to come across

What I've been longing for

Statues of God *ILLUSION*

One day
Out of faith welling up from your heart
To search for the truth of God
You decide to visit holy places, temples and churches all over the world
And set out on a journey

One year and then another passes
You have studied multitudes of holy texts
You have seen countless pictures and sculptures of God
Still your restless search for God urges you to the next temple

But your money is spent
You cannot buy food let alone afford a place to rest

Utterly exhausted
You eventually collapse halfway through your journey
Unable to see and senses receding
You lie on the roadside 'like a dead person'
Gaunt and in tatters with no one paying any attention

Just then
A man comes up to you and takes your hand
He lifts you in his arms and carries you to his shabby bunk
Then he shares with you his water and half-eaten bread

Living from hand to mouth, he is a poor man with no job
And furthermore he follows no religion or faith
He is a man of no education or culture and has never even thought about God

Naturally, it does not occur to him that you are travelling in search of God
And have fallen ill on the road but he simply cannot ignore you lying on the street
So he is taking every possible care of you

While he carries you in his arms and gives water through your dry lips
You watch him with a vacant gaze and think:

"It is all by the grace of God"
"God has saved my life through this poor man"

As if the man who is actually giving you water and bread has not come into view
Thinking of the pictures and statues of God you saw in many temples and churches
You simply give your thanks to them

But did the pictures and statues of God you prayed to
Give you even a single drop of water when you collapsed?

In order to survive, is not what you need the most
The bread and water the uneducated and faithless man has given you?
Yet you turn your eyes away from this truth

The true light of God is in the kindness of this man who is taking care of you

God is

His arms helping you rise up from the roadside
His hands moistening your dry lips with water

Also
His feelings of compassion
And his gestures of compassion in trying to save your life are indeed the signs of God

God

Can be found in a person's kindness and compassion

If you can feel gratitude
Toward all things

Then God's presence

Can be found not only in people but also in the blessings of all things

Normally, you take for granted your clothes, your daily food and your home
But when you feel gratitude for these things
You will come to understand this is the quickest way to know God's blessings

Then it will bring love and joy
Which you can never get from idle pictures or statues of God

The long hours you have spent
The many miles you have walked in quest of God
Will come to an end at this point

You no longer have to visit
Many temples and churches in search of God

As God

Can be found right by your side
And in your heart
No matter where you are or what you do

The Moon *CONSCIENCE*

If your body is compared to a glass
The water poured into the glass would be your soul and life itself

God shimmers in your heart like the moon reflected on the water, which is you

Whether the glass that is your body
Is of low quality or of high value
The reflection of the moon will have the same colour and shape
Whether it is a small glass or as large as a swimming pool
There is only one moon reflected on the surface of water

God gives equal blessings to all living things

To the weak and strong, to the ugly and beautiful
To the poor and rich, and to those who are foolish and those who are not
God's true image is always retained

As for the water
The purer and more transparent it is
The more it reflects the radiance of the moon deep below the surface

Likewise, the more honest and purer your soul is
The more clearly in its depth
Can you discover the real image of God

Like the moon reflected more as it is
When the water surface is calmer and the waves fewer

If you have found the meaning of love in your life
And even at times of anxiety or of sorrow
You do not forget gratitude and compassion while keeping a kind heart

Then within your own soul, you will be able to see the image of God

Turbid water
Cannot reflect the moon's radiance deep below its surface

If you cannot feel joy and forget your conscience as a person
Or if you are swayed by your ego, you will not be able to see God

The waving surface of water
Gradually distorts the reflection of the moon

If your heart is in pain due to sorrow and anxiety
Or always swayed by hatred and anger
Your soul will billow and stir
And the image of God will look distorted in your eyes

Like the moonlight streaming down on the earth
God gives love to everyone alike

You are the water reflecting the moonlight
If your soul has conscience

God is your reflection in the mirror
And is the very image of love that has become one with you

Flowing Water HEART

Flowing water is pure, fresh, clear and beautiful

People will want to bathe in such water
And have no hesitation in drinking it

But once this flowing water
Stops moving and turns into ditchwater that has ceased to flow
It will in time become turbid, stagnant, mossy and harbour microbes and wigglers
Then people will no longer want to drink such water or bathe in it

If one's heart
Constantly moves and changes like flowing water
It will retain its liveliness and beauty

A drop of rainwater constantly changes its form
After falling on the ground and before flowing into the sea
It becomes a dewdrop on a leaf, a purling brooklet flowing through rocks
A stream moistening the fields and then a large river flowing leisurely through land

Likewise, a person's heart
From the moment of birth in this world until death and returning to Mother God
Goes through many changes

Joy, sorrow, hope, despair, anger, tenderness, fear, courage, goodwill, malice
Love, hatred, peace of mind, anxiety, jealousy, triumph, friendship...
A person's heart responds in thousands of different ways

Becoming richer as it changes form and colour
Like water retaining its beauty by constantly flowing
A person's heart retains its beauty by constantly changing

It is like blood
By constant circulation
Sustaining life through the body's metabolism

Like the bloodstream maintaining life in your body
The constant changes occurring in your heart prove that you are alive

Like a morning glory with petals turning red and purple with the colour of water
A person's heart can be tinged with the colour of happiness or misery

If you only persists in your own joy
And do not care about the worries and miseries of others
Your heart would seem like turbid water containing poison

Flowers blooming in poisonous water turn into sad and lonely flowers loved by no one

But if your heart
Does not fear changes such as joy and sorrow, and stays strong and supple
Then you would be a lively, healthy and happy person loved by everyone

You would be like a beautiful flower always blooming in fresh and clear water

Tears Falling *FREEDOM*

You constantly worry about controlling others
Not relaxing even for the briefest moment
And never free from tension

Still more when it comes to controlling your own heart
You probably think that it requires
Tremendous energy and patience

In order to control your heart
Would you erase your emotions?

Or would you
Try changing your heart forcibly?
Perhaps your interpretation of controlling your heart

Is to become someone who is not yourself

> What can you do with fear surging up inside you?
> What can you do with tears trickling down your cheeks?
> What can you do with your irreplaceable smile?
> What can you do with blessings welling up within you?

You need not go against rushes of emotions
Joy, sorrow, suffering and kindness
Any emotion
Is proof of the life force naturally surging through your heart

All you have to do
Is to be true to yourself as a person

Being true to yourself
Is to care about others' feelings
Never leaving out compassion for other things
It is also about following your conscience

So if your heart is always in a state of conscience
Controlling your heart is something you need not even think about

    Sleep naturally, dream naturally, awake naturally
    Laugh naturally, cry naturally
    Love naturally and be loved naturally...

    The joy of living naturally

    How wonderful it is to live like that!

If you listen to your conscience and live honestly as a person
Then like the clear sky
You will be loved and cared for by everyone

All you have to do is to set your heart free

Mirror *SECRET*

When you see your angry face reflected in a mirror
You will not find it frightening
Because it is your own face and you know you are angry

But if you suddenly show your angry face to another person
Then that person will find it frightening
Because it is not that person's own face nor does that person know you are angry

If you see your crying face reflected in the mirror
You will not be surprised
Because it is your own face and you know you are crying

But if you suddenly show your crying face to another person
Then that person will probably be surprised
Because it is not that person's own face nor does that person know you are crying

However, when you show your angry face or crying face to God
God will neither be frightened nor surprised

Because
You are an embodiment of God and God is always with you
God knows everything about you even when you shed a secret tear

CHAPTER 2

The Ego
FOOL

In the hustle-bustle of the city

You were the only one in view

That summer night

The Ego   *FOOL*

Opening an umbrella in the light
Will form one small shadow beneath the umbrella

Folding the umbrella
Will let the shadow disappear without a trace and only infinite light will remain

Seawater can be held in one's hands if it is poured inside a small glass
Pouring it back from the glass to the sea will instantly make it turn into the ocean

A soul lodging in an animate being
Dies and becomes one with an infinite soul called God

But we have created 'egos'
By possessing bodies with various forms and appearances

Many of us have forgotten
That we and other things are actually one

Our body is the umbrella and is also the same as the glass

'The Ego' from God's point of view

Is like opening an umbrella on a sunny day
Or like carefully holding a small glass filled with seawater while on a ship

And it is meaningless
It is also foolish not to see the infinite light or the vast expanse of ocean

Prayers *DESIRE*

In some uncultivated jungles
Offerings for gods are not only fish and beasts
Sometimes even humans are dedicated as sacrifices

We who live in industrialized countries
Would never think of believing in such gods
Or even regard them as gods

But those who live in such jungles
Believe that their gods are the most sublime

In their prayers
They often ask for victory in their wars and battles

They sometimes pray to kill opposing tribes
Or to burn down their villages
Their prayers as such can be cruel and brutal

And the gods they believe in
Grant the wishes of those who have sacrifices to offer
Even if they were to cause damage to others

Then those gods are no longer godlike but should be regarded as devils

We who live in more civilised modern societies
Would easily understand that
Those are not true prayers let alone a true prayer to God

But let us think again
Peoples' prayers take thousands of different forms

In your prayers
You may have wished for many evil desires
Like those performed in uncultivated jungles

You may have forgotten
To care about others in your wishes

Just a few decades ago during the Second World War

People living in today's civilised nations
Or countries already regarded as civilised back then
Might in effect have been praying for the fall of the opposing countries
For the victory of their nation

Though different in style
They might have been the same as prayers in the uncultivated jungles

In your current prayer
Your heart may not care
What happens to others as long as your own wish is granted

If your prayers and wishes are about
Becoming happier and richer than others

In other words, if your wish is about
Being 'better off than others'
Then your prayer cannot be called a true prayer to God

You who cannot feel the joys of life
Unless you compare yourself with others may be called a foolish person

Though the food you are eating may be enjoyable
When you see the person next to you eating something that looks even better
You may suddenly feel that your food does not taste as good

When your friend's house seems luxurious and spacious
Your own house may begin to make your life feel miserable

When you compare a present from your love
With a present your friend received
You may feel that you are unlucky because it is not as classy or expensive

You feel relieved when you see someone less fortunate than yourself
You feel dejected when you see someone more fortunate than yourself

You may have forgotten to care for those who are unfortunate
And have decided that you are an unfortunate person

You may have prayed for selfish desires
Requiring the sacrifice of other people

One that grants such selfish desires is not a god but a devil

The act of praying to a devil
Is the same as asking a black-hearted and greedy person to grant your wish
And you will end up having to pay a price many times bigger

If you pray with a heart that is selfish and lacks compassion
God will not be there for you

But if your wish is not some comparison with others
And if you pray with a heart full of love for peace

Then no matter how trivial or no matter how difficult
Or no matter how much miracles your wish may require
It will be granted and be blessed by God

Flowers in a Meadow   *WAVE*

Flowers growing in meadows are beautiful
You are in the sun and love to watch flowers blooming gloriously

Then you pick a flower
Because you want to keep the flower's beauty all for yourself

But the flower in your hand has lost its breath of life
And the beauty of the flowers you saw swaying in the wind has faded away

A pony running around in a field chasing a butterfly
Looks like an innocent angel

Then you
Capture the pony and put it behind a fence

But the captured pony
Has already lost its angel-like gaze
And no trace of its beauty full of vitality is left

You are in love
Your heart flutters when you see your love's casual gestures and little smiles
You try to imagine what is being said although you hear no voice

Then you begin to live with your love
Wanting to keep this person all to yourself

But still
You want more and more possession
Your heart no longer flutters
Even when you see your love's casual gestures or little smiles
You no longer try to imagine what is being said although you still hear no voice

Intellect, Desires and Devils *INTELLIGENCE*

Most animals' behavioural patterns are determined by
The desire to eat, the desire to sleep and the desire for sex

They are basic desires to sustain life and to create offspring
They are by no means a product of intellect

Human behaviour is determined
Not only by these basic desires
But in many cases by various desires of the intellect

Human behaviour
Is by far more complex and strange compared to non-human animals
Because man has intellect incomparable to other animals

And
Desires caused by intellect are endless
As they keep on emerging

You are watching television
When you see a car commercial, you want to buy a new car
When you watch a drama, you want to live like the heroine

You are walking on the streets
When you see lovers pass by, you want to fall in love
When you see a nice row of houses on a street, you want to live there

Every person has
Basic desires from birth
They are genuine desires of the body

The level of satisfaction is relevant to physical satisfaction
It can be fulfilled naturally

As for desires caused by intellect

Which are
Desires caused by knowing there is something else
The level of satisfaction can be measured only in each person's mind

Moreover, when a person's desire is fulfilled
It only leads to an even bigger desire

Let's say you have bought clothes that you like
You are satisfied then, but when you see someone wearing better clothes

You might even feel embarrassed to wear the ones you have bought
And want new clothes again

Let's say you have built a house
For the first couple of years, you are satisfied to own a house of your choice

But around the third year, you might start craving for an even bigger house

You are no longer satisfied with your current house
And your desire to live in a new house gets stronger day by day

There is no end to man's desires

Because man has the ability to know
And there is no end to desires caused by constant curiosity about new things

Intellect can be frightening
It has the power to change current contentment to discontent

People's hearts tend to be very greedy

They want to actually see what they read and hear
They want to touch what they see, possess what they touch
And they want to keep it all to themselves

Once they have done so
Just like a child who is bored with his new toy right away and wants another one
They feel new desires

The numerous wars that took place in history
Were perhaps all for the sake of
Fulfilling the desires of individuals or nations

You may say that very many of man's mistakes
Are due to desires caused by intellect

From ancient to medieval times when slavery and class systems existed
People were not allowed to have intellect
Except for those in power and their aides
They could not defy their rulers and were forced to labour

Warriors died in battlefields not even knowing the cause of their war

Humanity
Lies in the wonderful fact that people can have more than the basic desires

But slaves and warriors
Were not even given the right to know
Nor were they able to fully satisfy their basic desires to protect their lives

And today
When everyone has been given the right to know
A new type of misery is threatening mankind

In the midst of
A kaleidoscope of information sweeping past us like a storm
Man's intellect is giving birth to new desires
More quickly than ever before

To know many things has created much discontent
People compare themselves with others and feel unhappy

Unfulfilled desires make some people give up their lives and others commit crimes

If there is nothing to question the right and wrong of desires
People would have free rein to their desires

They may become heartless
Using any means to achieve their aims

This might cause yet another tragic war
Making people hurt each other

A society controlled merely by intellect and desires
Could turn out to be a very devilish world

Devils are full of intellect
They act promptly and even very rationally

But there is one thing that devils lack
This thing is 'reason'

Reason is indeed
The great power to make people question whether their desires are right or wrong

CHAPTER 3

To Love
WORDS

Just before winter   The sky is clear

The time I spend with you is worth eternity

To Love   *WORDS*

You know

Sorrow because you have a heart
And joy because you have a heart

But you will not be able to reply if asked where your heart is

Because

The heart is not a place to think
The heart is something that fills up naturally
The heart is not something unchangeable like an immovable stone
The heart is something that changes like flowing water

You may say

You do not know how to find your heart
But you do not need to know how to find your heart

Your heart

Is yourself
And like you who was given life because of love
Your heart was also created by love

All the feelings

Coming through your heart cannot be spoken without love
Every single word is born from love

For instance 'beauty'—You do not learn about love from beauty
You learn about beauty by loving

For instance 'courage'—You do not learn about love by having courage
You learn about courage by loving

For instance 'sorrow'—You do not learn about love by sorrow
You learn about sorrow by loving

For instance 'sympathy'—You do not learn about love because you have sympathy
You learn about sympathy by loving

For instance 'kindness'—You do not learn about love by being kind
You learn about kindness by loving

To know courage by loving
To know fear by loving
To know joy by loving
To know distress by loving
To know love by loving

To know our children by loving
To know our parents by loving
To know our friends by loving
To know tender passion by loving
To know God by loving

Love is the standard
Of all the feelings inside your heart and all the words that exist in the world

    Hatred is a word used when you cannot love others
    Sorrow is a word used when you cannot love yourself

Only when you love

Will words naturally reach the heart
And you will know even spiritual awakening, truth and God by loving

Love and Desire   *BLUE*

You want to love your life

You already know that being able to love your life
Is indeed the happiest thing of all

In order to love your life
You think that various desires have to be satisfied
So you try to realise the desires welling up inside you

Greed for money, ambition for fame
Desire for sole possession, desire for ownership and various carnal desires...

You try hard
Believing that you can love life at its most
The moment you satisfy your desultory desires

But
Once you know that it is impossible to fulfill your desires
You curse not only your desires
But even life itself

You love yourself so much
That life seems miserable

To love yourself
And to love life is similar but different

Those who only love themselves forget the meaning of love

You may have confused love and desire

The feeling you have for your lover
Could be the desire for sole possession or the desire for ownership

You may think
Love is like desire

In what is not satisfied there is no point
In what is not satisfied there is nothing but bitterness

So you may be afraid of loving
As you are expecting something in return just as you do from desires

Desires
Become yours when they are satisfied but disappear on that very moment

As for love
It will become yours forever just by loving even if it is not satisfied

    Love is not the wish to be loved
        Nor the desire to be loved

    Love is merely to love—it is that simple

Love will become yours undeniably just by loving

One could say
You love your life to the fullest
When you have found true love

True love is to love something other than yourself
So much that it makes you forget your own desires

That is when
You will be able to love your own life

You may, for instance, love your work from your heart
And devote yourself entirely to your work even forgetting your own interests
Then you will be able to find a life that you love

Even if
You lose your loved one or something dear to you
The joy of having met someone you love or encountering something dear to you

Would take away
Your desultory desires and erase them
And bring pure joy to your life

In order to make your life full of love
All you have to do is to become a person
Who can love things other than yourself

Separation   FOREVER

Love may fill your life with joy
Love may fill your life with sorrow

But those who do not know love may be even more unfortunate

When you lose someone you love
Whether by death or separation
You will probably be overwhelmed by sorrow

But your sorrow
Proves that your love was true

It proves that the deeper your sorrow, the deeper your love
And the longer your sorrow, the more eternal your love is

So when you are so grief-stricken and are on the verge of collapse
You should think like this:

  I am proud because I have experienced true love

I am grateful
For the joy of meeting my loved one
And for discovering happiness through true love

When you
Part with your love
Yet feel little sorrow or pain
Then your life will be meagre, hollow and boring

Even the happy days in your memory
Will fade away rapidly in no time

Rather than to spend a life
Without knowing true love, true joy and true sorrow

To know true love and to lead a life to the fullest
Even in the midst of true joy and sorrow
Would be such a wonderful thing

If you discover true love in your life
Then after the sorrow
You will surely find beaming joy once again

Existence   *GRATITUDE*

If you are all alone in this world
You will not even be aware of your own existence

You may be a wise person
But there will be no one to recognise that

You may be a person of justice
But there will be no one to help

You may be beautiful
But you will not know other faces

You may know words
But there will be no one to talk to

You are...
You are...
You are...

Although you are no doubt alive
There is no way to tell that you are alive

If there is nothing that meets your eyes
You will think that you do not need eyes

If there is no one to listen to your stories
You will think that you do not need a mouth

If there is no one to clasp hands with
You will think that you do not need hands

If you are all alone in the dark universe
You might even think that you do not need your life

If there is someone to look back into your eyes
You will feel grateful to your eyes

If there is someone to listen to your stories
You will feel grateful to your mouth

If there is someone to clasp hands with
You will feel grateful to your hands

If you are surrounded by things that have life
You will realise the importance of your own life

When your eyes look at things other than yourself
When your mouth talks to things other than yourself
And when your hands touch things other than yourself
That is when the feeling of being alive returns to your heart

You will be grateful to each part of your body
To all the things you see, hear, talk to and touch
And treat every single word with respect

You will cherish your eyes, mouth and hands...
And will try to fill your whole body with the joy of being alive

You will hate a mouth that lies
You will hate eyes that lack a gentle look
You will hate hands that lack compassion
You will hate yourself for not knowing love

You will want every part of your precious body to overflow with gestures of love

Happiness by Chance GENTLY

You may
Be lamenting that
Your unexpected misfortune is a quirk of fate

And you may think that
Your happiness is due to your own efforts
But never admit it is due to God's benevolence

You believe only in yourself as you cannot believe in God

You cannot even believe in love
And you are convinced that everything is turning against you

You think
Happiness cannot be found just by waiting
And say all happiness should have a purpose

You say there is no need to choose means in order to achieve happiness

You say there is no time to care about others
Nor to look back at yourself

For you
Kindness leads to decadence
And when people say they want to be happy

You say
With triumph and severity
That they have to experience hardships like you have

You do not dare
Think of thanking God
For the happiness you have achieved by fair means or foul
Nor for the happiness you might have derived at times

You do not even care that happiness lacking gratitude is not true happiness

That is why
Other people's happiness always bothers you and you cling to your own
Never trying to share your happiness with others

But you have a friend
Who is always smiling and is liked by everyone
He always seems to be enjoying his life

And above all, he looks happier than you are

You will
Probably hate his smile
And hate him for enjoying happiness without experiencing hardships

You will hate to see him sharing his happiness with others and being loved by them

He does not intend to have a fixed idea of what happiness is

He loves others just as he loves himself
And at times devotes himself to others selflessly

Yet he is not bothered by hardships
And he never ceases to smile

He is grateful
For each moment of happiness
Thinking he does not deserve to be blessed with such happiness

He sincerely wants to share his happiness with many people

God
Loves your friend just as your friend loves others

God
Wishes your friend to be happy just as your friend wishes other people's happiness

God
Exists in the mirror reflecting you

When your heart reaches across to God and becomes one with God's heart
The seeds of happiness will fall upon you

As if by chance
As though you are breathing

Happiness will visit you quite naturally

It will never
Surprise you like a miracle nor will it make a display of its wonder

You are the only one who will notice it
And it will settle in your life naturally

You will be genuinely grateful for the happiness God has sent you
You will never become fixated if you feel gratitude
And you will learn the joy of sharing such happiness with many people

True happiness will never visit you
Without the feeling of gratitude
This you will certainly come to know

Match Flame *SUNLIGHT*

    In the middle of the night
    The little flame of a match lit in a vast playing field
    Can be seen clearly in the depth of darkness

  At dusk
  The match flame can only be seen vaguely
  And in broad daylight
  Hardly anyone will notice
  The match flame in the playing field

When people are veiled in deep sorrow
They learn to appreciate the little acts of compassion
  That they do not usually notice
  When their sorrow is only half-serious
    People by and large do not even understand the meaning of compassion

  So perhaps the more fortunate the person is
    The more they tend to forget
      Compassion

You might be
    An unhappy person
        But even if you cannot do anything for them
            By understanding the hearts of others lost in darkness
            Your feeling of compassion
            Will become the light of love
        For the person lost in deep sorrow
    Just like the sunlight
Shining in the tacit universe

CHAPTER 4

Nature
GOD

The rain   Hands held out

Reflecting my face   Mirror of Nature   Filling my palms

The Sea *MOTHER*

On earth
There are countless rivers and all river waters flow constantly

Rivers flow
Because their waters have a place to go to

The sea
Contains water incomparable to rivers in volume
It also
Accepts waters from any river unconditionally

Countless rivers
Flow into each other
And in due course, all rivers arrive at the sea

Like the sea not tinged with any colour ink dropped into its waters

A river
No matter how turbid its flow may be
Will become the sea's transparent colour when it returns to the sea

To a river
The sea must be sacred water, infinite love and ultimately Mother God

Your soul
Must be able to follow through your life
Because it has a place to go to

Your soul
Also flows right into Mother God like a river

It is a large soul incomparable to yours in size
Yet also
This vast soul accepts you unconditionally

As long as
You are not afraid and do not reject it
It will purify you with its lucent love

God would never reject you just like the sea never rejecting river waters

The Sea's Destination   REINCARNATION

The sea
   Bathes in sunlight
   Turns into invisible vapour and then into clouds

The seawater
   Becomes the celestial sea and appears in the sky again

When the clouds
   Hide the sun, people cannot see the sun
   But the clouds know that the sun is always shining above them

The celestial sea
   Soon becomes the rain and falls on this land
   The rain falling to the ground will forget it was once in the celestial sea

   The rain will forget it was once a cloud
   The clouds will forget they were once the sea
   The sea will forget it was once a river
   The river will forget it was once the rain

   But
   Nature would never forget
   As
   Nature is watching eternally

Like the sea
   Cradling life under its gentle waves

God
   Cradles our soul in gentle love

The soul
   As if it cannot wait to start a new life
   Becomes a cloud or the rain to return to this world

The sun
   Hears the first cry of new life in the strong light during the day
   And becomes the moonlight luring our souls to peaceful sleep at night

The soul
   Returns to God, forgets its past lifetime and waits
   To set out on a new life's journey, protected by God as if in its mother's arms

However
   The soul has no way to know where it is heading for

   The river does not know it will become the sea
   The sea does not know it will become a cloud
   The clouds do not know they will become the rain
   The rain does not know it will become a river

   But
   Nature knows
   Because
   Nature exists in eternal repetition

The clouds
  Are carried by the wind

The wind
  Is air that flows to places where air is scarce

The sky
  Is God itself and love itself

The wind
  Carries the clouds to where God's blessings are scarce
  To where God's love is scarce

The clouds
  Turn into rain there

The rain
  Becomes God's love and new life after a while
  Changing into flowers, trees, the earth, birds and beasts...

People
  Become the flowing river
  And the flow of blessed water

God
  Dreams of you becoming the love of nature itself

The Air *LOVE*

The air seems like nothing at first glance

Is it a place that all existences share?
Or is it something that provides everything a place to exist?

You are inside a bright light
You say there is nothing in between you and me facing each other like this
This is because you have forgotten
That we are looking at each other across the air

You say you cannot see my face in the dark
Because the darkness gets in the way
This is because
You have forgotten that we are looking at each other across the air

The air

Is not darkness and as the air is transparent
It only reflects light during the day and darkness at night

You may think you cannot possess the air
For you cannot grasp the air
You may think you cannot do as you please with the air
For you cannot fly in the air

But you know that you cannot breathe without air

Whether you are wise or foolish
A person of justice or of malice, beautiful or ugly

The air

      Enters you without discrimination
      And everyone inhales and exhales the same air equally

In this room
Even if you hate me
You still inhale the breath I exhale
I inhale the breath you exhale
You and I are breathing each other's breath

When you are in a meadow
The animals and plants inhale the breath you exhale
And you inhale the breath exhaled by the animals and plants

The air

      Flows inside all things equally
      You cannot grasp the air
      But you are always absorbing the air inside your body
      Far more deeply than by laying your hands on it

The air

      Becomes the clear blue sky, the red sunset and the colours of the rainbow
      And you can see it whenever you want to

The air would neither escape nor hide from you
No matter what kind of person you are

When you look up
You can see exactly the same sky as everyone else

The air

      To people, animals, flowers and grass...
      Is fair to all things and is free

If until now you have never thanked the air
It is because you have never thought about the necessity of the air

If you still cannot thank the air

It is because you want to receive kindness just for yourself
          You want to receive special treatment just for yourself

It is almost like
A baby not realising his mother's caring

Just like a suckling baby
Taking his mother's breasts for granted

The air

    Is your mother
    And the mother of all things
    The air is the very image of God's love

The Air II *BREATH*

Even if your heart
Is unable to thank God that is the air
Your body
Knows very well that the air is God's blessing and the food of life

To prove this
When you are hurling abuse or shouting at someone aloud
Your whole body trembles with anger
And you breathe out the air with incredible energy

Your heart beats fast
Only intermittently can you breathe the air
And you may even fall ill due to grief and agony

This is because through rage, grief and agony
You are shutting out the air that is God

When you smile
You inhale and then exhale the air
Very easily and naturally

And when you are laughing out loud
You are inhaling and exhaling the air in plenty
It must be a happy moment for your mind and body

God becomes the air
Given unconditionally to all things and is always with you

By breathing
You once contain and then release God

If your heart is pure
In other words, if your heart can be called your conscience
Then your words will express God's aspects

God
Dwells in a person's body
And is embodied through that person's words and gestures

The air becomes the food of life
That is, as long as you appreciate God's blessings and do not forget love
Anyone can naturally become the embodiment of God

Saints *BIG RIVER*

The rain
Falls on the fields
Enters a seed and becomes a flower

A flower
Cannot move from place to place
But gives comfort to those who see it

A beast
Perhaps lives only to eat
But it also falls prey to other animals
And become their food of life

People
Are like blessed rivers
Streams join together and become a river
A big river will engulf a small river with its voluminous waters
Forming one great river flowing into the sea

Hieroglyphically
The Chinese character for 'people' resembles that of 'river'
Three rivers join together and become one big river
People help and care for each other
They come together with a single purpose, give birth to love and nurtures it

Mahatma Gandhi, Mother Teresa
The Prophet Muhammad, Jesus Christ, Gautama Buddha...

All the saints
Have shared their love impartially
Like the flow of a great river
They have carried countless rivers to the divine ocean

None of the saints
Spared love or were selective
That is simply how they were

Nature   GOD

You are a tree

You are one big tree growing luxuriantly in a forest
Many birds perch on your branches
They eat your fruit and then begin to nest

Many years have gone by and you have endured much wind and rain
As you have grown old, you can hear the birds singing only in the far distance

You eventually rot off and turn into soil

Then instead of the songs of the birds
You hear footsteps of various animals walking on your body
And feel the rainwater flowing inside your body

That is when you know you have turned into soil

As you grow fertile
Insects lay eggs
Larvae hatch, take you in as nourishment and crawl around on the ground

You know you have become an insect

And then
A bird sweeps down from the sky to peck you and you enter the bird's body
You fly high in the boundless sky
Listen to the sound of the wind and see various landscapes new to you
When you look down at the world below your eyes

You know you have become a bird

Then
You find a tree towering in a forest
You peck the fruit on its boughs and before long begin to nest

Reincarnation
Is not just something happening on the axis of time

Various states of reincarnation can be witnessed
Within the dimensions of this world

All things
Exist for the sake of all and help each other

All things have various forms derived from one soul
They share the same soul but their roles differ depending on the body they dwell in

Just like
The hands, feet, eyes, mouth and ears of your body

All elements of nature existing in the universe
Are various forms created from one heart

And you can say
That this heart is not just God's heart
But also God's embodiment

Life of Nature COSMOS

A person is made up of 60 trillion cells
And each cell
Is trying desperately to survive
The different functions of each cell sustain a person's life

Human beings
Is the generic name given to a collective body comprised of such 60 trillion cells

Supposing you are a microcosm
Then all 60 trillion cells live inside your cosmos
They are your life itself comprising your microcosm
Likewise
Creatures living in this magnificent world of nature
Humans including yourself
Fish, birds, beasts, grasses, flowers, trees, the earth, the moon, the sun, other planets...
All things that exists
Are life forms of nature that make up nature and also nature itself

You look up at the heavens and ask God
  "God, who am I?
   God, do you know me?
   God, please reveal yourself to me."
It is as if
You are being asked by one of the cells inside your body
How would you answer
These questions asked by one little cell inside you?

"If I am God
Then you and I are the same embodiment of God.
You are one of the life forms of God that makes me exist.
You were born with me and you are with me just as you are now.
I cannot reveal myself to you
Because
You are always with me.
If you still want to see me as God
All you have to know is that
Everything you see with your eyes is what I am.
All things that exist are one just like you and me."
That might be the only answer you can give to your cell

If you are a microcosm
And your cells are the life forms making up the microcosm
God is then the macrocosm
And you are a life form of God that makes up God

And God
Can be referred to as everything that exists
From far beyond the macrocosm to the place right by your feet

That is
What Nature is
You are the Life of Nature and Nature itself

CHAPTER 5

Anticipation of a Renaissance
OLD & NEW

A starless night

I want you to know   There is a sky full of stars above the clouds

Anticipation of a Renaissance   OLD & NEW

The earth

Is one of the planets
Moving in a certain orbit within the solar system
Mankind's discovery of this fact
Is very recent when compared to mankind's long history

In the past

Man never imagined the earth was a sphere
It was considered that the world rested on an elephant's back
And that there was a huge waterfall at the end of the sea
These things were common beliefs

And now

Scholars have at last begun to understand
The relation between the earth and other planets, satellites and comets
And the rules of the universe

At present

Everyone knows about the existence of the earth and the universe
That the earth moves round the sun in about 365 days
And rotates once on its axis in about 24 hours

    And that the moon

Revolves round the earth in about 29 days and takes 29 days to rotate on its axis
Therefore we can only ever see
One side of the moon

                                                 The ebb and flow of the tides

                     Occurs due to the relative positions of the moon and the earth
                            The tide flows when the moon's gravitation increases
                            The tide ebbs when the moon's gravitation lessens

    And when Mars draws near the earth
It is said that abnormal weather occurs

                                                       So it has become clear

                                  That the earth is influenced in many ways
                                  Due to its position in relation to other stars

    Likewise
Man are also influenced by other stars and the moon

"The earth is blue"

This is a famous comment by the Soviet cosmonaut Gagarin
As it is true that 70% of the earth is covered by sea
70% of the human body is also made up of water

    Our sweat tastes salty like seawater
    The specific gravity of seawater and that of human body fluid
    Are both approximately 1.03

    Like the ebb and flow of the tides caused by the moon's gravitation
A person is likely to be born when the tide is high and die when the tide is low

    According to statistics
On nights with a full moon, the crime rate increases to an extreme level

    Perhaps Saki's famous novel 'Gabriel-Ernest'
About a boy transforming into a werewolf became a bestseller worldwide
Because people
Unconsciously realised
The strange power of the full moon

    Like the rotation and revolution of the moon
    Women's menstrual cycles
    Are around 29 days

    The moon and stars may be influencing man
In many other ways

                              Western astrology
                              Is based on statistics using the relative positions of the stars

                                          When science was still undeveloped

                It was born as a result of finding some cause in the relation between
                        Man and the operations and positions of the moon and stars
                              By observing the destinies of many people

        In sustaining the life of the earth

One of the important things is gravity
Both the moon and the earth have gravitation
And all the stars affect one another because they all have gravity

                                                      Gravity

                                Is something you can neither see nor touch
                                    However, its existence and influence
                                        Has been confirmed in many ways

      As the gravity of the stars

Establishes the rules of the universe
The soul could be compared to gravity directing man's destiny

                                  The soul is like gravity

                                        You can neither see nor touch it
                                But it could be deeply related to man's destiny

      Like gravity becoming gravitation

Like stars joining together to form galaxies
And like galaxies joining together to form the universe

                                              The soul is perhaps
                           Connected to all life by its invisible force

    The direction you believe to be east

Could be west or it could be south
When observed from one point in the universe
Because the earth is continuously rotating and revolving

                            What you have learned

                And what you firmly believe could be merely trivia
                          Within the truth of the universe

    Like astronomers

Who solve mysteries of the universe
Perhaps we too have to search for the rules of our souls

                          Like the destiny of the stars

              Entrusted to the galaxy and thus to the entire universe
           People's destiny is perhaps due to the providence of Nature

Soul and Body RULE

The relation between the soul and the body in a person's lifetime
Can be compared to the relation between a person and a house

Your soul can be compared to you
And your body to the house you live in

Just as you live in your house
Your soul dwells in your body

Just as your house
Is limited in its size, status and location
Due to your economic, domestic and social conditions

Your body's
Parentage, appearance and capacity are selected
Due to various conditions and restrictions placed on your soul

Because of various conditions and restrictions
You might not be able to live in an ideal house

Likewise, it is very unlikely that your soul
Dwells in an ideal body because of various restrictions

This can be understood
From the fact that when you were born in this world
You did not choose your lineage, legal domicile, appearance or talent

The moment your soul enters your body, that is when you give your first cry at birth
You are given a body to dwell in according to 'restrictions on your soul'

Such restrictions on the soul are called 'karma' or 'causation' in Buddhist terms

But even if you are
Not satisfied with various things about yourself

Such as your background, appearance, personality, talent or health
And stricken with grief and agony, you should never give up

By changing your state of mind
You can change yourself in any way you like

For instance
If there is someone who cannot feel joy in life

And even when at home
Continues to be grief-stricken

This person will not feel like cleaning the house
And leave repair work undone

A house owned by such person will become more and more damaged
And it will crumble and fall into ruins as if many decades have passed

The body might be like a house
If your heart dwelling in your body is unable to find joy
And merely repeats a pattern of grief and agony

Then your body will weaken and suffer from illnesses and woes

Like mental frustration and strain making blood circulation irregular
And causing a heart attack

A person's state of mind
Causes illness more often than you think

You may be fortunate and have a very healthy body due to your soul's condition
But if your heart cannot find peace of mind
Your body might become unhealthy

The face of a person who plays foul, untrue and false
The face of a person who is filled with hatred, envy and anger
And the face of a person seized with despair, anxiety and sorrow
None of them are beautiful

Likewise, no matter
How beautiful you were born
If you have the wrong attitude, your face will appear ugly

If the person living in a house is gloomy like darkness
Then the house will rapidly fall into decay

Likewise, if your mind is placed in darkness
Your body will collapse in no time

To leave your mind in an unsatisfied state
Is the same as giving ill-treatment to your body

On the contrary
If you are content with your life, have discovered joy in your work
And have also found joy in your relations with other people
Then your house will feel very comfortable

The windows will be wide open on a clear day
And the whole house will be filled with sunlight and fresh air

Such house will not seem old
But with a charm that only comes with history
It will turn into an even nicer and a comfortable place to live in

If your soul
Is filled with love, happiness, hope, joy and peace of mind
Then your body will also be free from illnesses and woes
And it will shine beautifully

Even if

You belittle your background
Worry about your poor health
Lack confidence in your appearance
And feel you have no talent

As long as your heart is filled with joy
And you can appreciate yourself just as you are
You will begin to shine beautifully

Everyone

Probably wants to look beautiful by birth
Be brought up in a rich and noble family
And be gifted with talents and a strong body

Unfortunately
Everything may differ from this ideal
But if you can love yourself just as you are and have a heart of joy
Then your life will surely begin to shine

On the other hand
Even if you are fortunate from the beginning of your life
Your life may turn into darkness if you do not have the right state of mind

Restrictions on the soul
May have been created by God

But your heart
Belongs to you
Whatever you may think and whatever you may feel

God will not go as far as to restrict your heart

Your heart

Is the infinite expanse of the sky that allows you to fly freely

Memories *POSSESSION*

The life one is given in this world
Can be rephrased as one's memories of this lifetime

To lose life in this world
In many cases, means losing the memories of this lifetime

All the people you came to know
Your parents, children, husband, wife, lover, friends...

Everything you experienced
Joy, sorrow, hope, peace, surprise...

You will lose all those memories

You loved, hated, laughed and wept
But all those memories will disappear from you
You will forget not only your face but also even your name
Perhaps that is what it means to rest in peace

If you are bound to memories of this world
Even after you have lost your body
You must be in so much distress that you do not know what to do
As if your whole body is bound and thrown into a field unable to move

After your soul has lost your body
If your memories alone remain as they are
It will create agony throughout all eternity

As you will not have a body
Your unfulfilled desires will become even stronger
And you might try to achieve your wishes
Even through the body of someone who is alive

Without a body, you will not be able to cry or express your anger
Nor will it allow you to die even if you wanted to and in those who are alive
You will try to plant your desires to be freed from eternal agony

When your life in this world ends
You should know that you are fortunate if you can go back to nothingness

Only by losing memories of this world
Can you experience the joy
Of having a following life in a new reincarnation

It is important to live the lifetime given to you
To find joy in your life
And not to spare any love or effort in your daily life

Possession   QUARK

It can be said that man's senses are functions of nerve cells in the cerebrum
Vision is the result of the cells forming the visual centre in the cerebrum
Analysing information that enters through the eyes

Moreover, brain cells have a wonderful function that instantly analyses information
Not only of things you are aware of but also of things you are not aware of

Let's say you are talking to me like this
Though you are naturally only aware of my face
You can actually also see the colours of my clothes and the curtain behind me
As well as various books in the bookcase and the coffee cup on the table

It is because, regardless of your awareness, your brain cells
Are instantly analysing and processing information
From everything entering your field of vision

This means that man's senses are products of cellular function
Whether you are aware of it or not
In other words, your thoughts and behaviours are determined by your cells

Thoughts and emotions triggered by the same cause differ depending on the person
Because each individual's cellular functions differ
Results of vision also differ due to the analytical capacity of the individual's brain cells
Or whether the cells are functioning normally or abnormally

According to one theory, the American Indians were unable to see his ship
When Christopher Columbus discovered the American continent

It may be because the Indians did not have a single clue of what ships were then
So their brain cells could not analyse
Any information of the ship that was in view

Also those who are mentally deranged or those who abuse drugs
Can see what is not in the field of vision, in other words, hallucinations
Probably due to abnormal analysis made by brain cells that have become abnormal

Sometimes, abnormal mental changes
Can be expressed by the word 'possession'
Are those whose brain cells have become deranged the only ones called the possessed?
If possession is due to some spiritual entity
The spiritual entity must also be a substance that has memory and thought energy

The cells of the human body are comprised of atoms
Moreover, the atoms are not solid but are comprised of a nucleus and electrons
The nucleus is also a collection of small substances called elementary particles
This is the discovery of modern science

Viewed in this light, you can say that a cell is a collection of elementary particles
And due to the functions of such numerous elementary particles
Man can sustain life, memorise and think

If the elementary particles of atoms in the cerebrum allow man to memorise and think
You can say that each elementary particle has memories and thoughts

If some elementary particles in your cerebrum were transplanted into my cerebrum
I would obtain the memories and thoughts of those elementary particles
And you would lose them

If those elementary particles contained the emotion of sadness
I might suddenly start crying

If they remembered an intense scene
I might see things that are not in my field of vision

The human body seemingly has no gaps in its form
But it is actually full of gaps when you observe it at the level of elementary particles
This may be why elementary particles can leave and enter the human body quite easily

Supposing elementary particles with memories and thoughts
Exist in space other than in the cellular atoms of the human body
And make up the air together with atoms and molecules
Then they might suddenly enter a human body

The human body is comprised of a huge amount of elementary particles
And the atoms that they make up
Keep balance and harmony
If different elementary particles enter the body
The function of the human cells that have maintained balance would start to go wrong
And cause disorder in the body's nerve cells and life-sustaining function

It might suddenly make you see things that you cannot possibly see
Hear what you cannot possibly hear
Recall memories you have never experienced or stir up incomprehensible feelings
And it could cause some physical disorder or illness of unknown origin

If the spiritual entity is an invisible substance with memories and thoughts
And elementary particles are indeed the identity of this invisible substance
Then the spiritual entity could be analysed scientifically and biologically

Possession could be the adverse mental and physical influence
Of such elementary particles

Errors and illnesses of unknown origin
Such as a father who has had no mental disorder
Suddenly killing his own child for no reason
Or a sudden attack of schizophrenia
Might be caused by the adverse effects of elementary particles

A recent trend of medical science is to study causes of illnesses
Not just from the cellular level but also from an even smaller microscopic level

Vital activity, in the final analysis
Is due to functions of atoms and molecules, and also elementary particles
Progress in medical science and further discoveries on the effects of elementary particles
Could bring many opportunities to find common ground with religion

The Universe and Time   0×60=60

The universe is constantly expanding
A river increases its width
Because it is constantly accepting new streams

The universe likewise may be accepting new things to flow into it

Just as one cannot see the exact moment of a person's growth
We may not be able to see the moment of the universe's expansion

People can only observe growth as an outcome
The universe's expansion also may only be observed as an outcome

People get fatter because they eat food
The universe also expands because it takes in some sort of energy

In order to identify the energy taken in by the universe
We will have to stop time and encounter the moment of its expansion

Naturally, the universe would stop expanding at that moment
And the sun, the earth and the stars of other galaxies would stop moving as well

At that precise moment when the universe expands, the universe is not expanding

However, it is at this exact moment
That the universe is taking in energy required for its expansion
This must be the time called 'moment'

When you make a thorough analysis of a moment
You will reach a state of complete stillness

A moment is a state of standstill
That is a state in which time has stopped

Time is created through the accumulation of stillnesses
It is like creating beings from nothing
Zero seconds accumulate and create numerical time

Instead of $0 \times 60 = 0$, it ticks away a time of 60

In a black hole
It could be $0 \times 60 = -60$ or even change to -600
Perhaps time transforms freely within things that exist

In the twentieth-century world of physical science
It was discovered that time carries energy
One of the famous discoveries is Einstein's theory of relativity

What is time?
People can perceive time because there is light and shadow

Objects in a photo do not move because light and shadow are printed on it
Photographs printed with light and shadow of a moment carry a time called 'moment'

Shadows are created by light
And light has shadows

A moment is created when light and shadow meet
Time flows
As light and shadow overlap and accumulate

Time can be regarded as
An accumulation of infinite energy
Of all things that existed, all things that exist and all things that will exist

The existence called 'the universe' may be continuing to expand
With the infinite energy of time

The big bang
Which is said to have created the universe

Is perhaps the operation of all things that existed
All things that exist
And all things that will exist

That carry infinite energy

CHAPTER 6

Little Dinosaurs
HUMAN BEINGS

Wind carries time, time changes into seasons

I am no longer in spring

Words *ISOLATION*

When the things I imagine in my right brain
Transform into words in my left brain
I feel irritated, as I cannot convey everything in my heart
I express my heart straining it through a sieve of words
I know that something is missing when I put my heart into words

No matter how much I love someone
When I put it into words, I can only say, "I love you very much"
But I know inside my heart
Exactly how I feel... how deep my love is...

Yet love is strained through a sieve of words and
There is no way to convey love that has sifted through

Since the moment mankind possessed words
We may have begun to lose something in exchange of this part of civilisation

Animals can understand each other though they do not have words
Fish, birds and beasts form groups in which to live

Besides communication within the same species
Fish, birds and beasts are able to escape from natural disasters beforehand
Perhaps they somehow have ways to to communicate with
Some part of Nature's intentions

Man, on the other hand
May have come to believe
They can only communicate properly with those who have words

Perhaps man began to create art because they knew unconsciously
The transience of the wind blowing through the gap between the heart and words

Art is a way to express a person's heart that cannot be put into words
People feel they can share their hearts through music and fine art
But it is different from Nature's senses

The part of mankind's heart that has been lost in exchange for words
Exists in the world of nature
It is probably only mankind
That has lost something important and become isolated from the rest of nature

Supernatural Power   *MELODY*

Birds and fish flee from earthquakes and volcanic eruptions before they occur
And can escape to safe places

Wild birds spend their life flying freely in the sky
But caged birds die when they are set free

In the past, people would lie stretched out on the ground
With the sound of the wind their pillow and rocks as their stool
Watching the setting sun

Now we avoid the smell of soil
Live on concrete
Sit on plastic chairs and watch TV

We avoid any dialogue with nature, pursue science
Shun our intuition and value logic
Ears that do not listen to the inner voice
Can only hear words spelled with the alphabet
And do not hear the voice of Nature

People used to be the children of Nature

And yet only man has greatly changed
From its innate state created by Nature, changing for good or bad
It is probably not erroneous to connect the progresses of mankind and science

But as a result, people have lost their intrinsic capacity
You may think this is a trifling matter
But it is like not being able to walk without shoes
Or like feeling unbearably insecure without medicine to cure illness
People have come to depend on the inventions of science

Like birds in a cage
People have forgotten how to fly and yet appear content

Birdcages are fortresses of science
And people now have great fear of anything unproven theoretically
This fear binds them even more to science

All that people do is to make the birdcages stronger
Yet their fear of the world outside grows even stronger

People are so absorbed in putting up barricades between themselves and Nature
That they have forgotten to dream of flying off into the infinite skies

Though science was born to solve the mysteries of natural phenomena
It is depriving humans of the discretionary power given to them by Nature

A bird in a cage used to be one of Nature's melodies cradled in nature
People, cradled in nature, have played Nature's melodies as well
And yet they do not listen to the voice of Nature
Nor hum the melody of Nature inside them

Little Dinosaurs   HUMAN BEINGS

Around 65.5 million years ago
Dinosaurs dominated the earth
There have been many controversies over the cause of their extinction
The most influential theory in recent years is
That a huge meteorite hit the earth

According to one scholar, a meteorite about 10 kilometres in diameter hit the earth
And not only were dinosaurs instantly driven to extinction
But so were most of the life forms that had existed during the Cretaceous period

Such mass extinction has happened not only to the dinosaurs
But also to a number of creatures that have appeared on the earth in the past
This point has been made clear through studies of fossils

Mass extinctions of living creatures, both large and small in scale
Have occurred regularly every 26 million years and 18 times in total
Beginning from trilobites 670 million years ago to ammonites and fusulinids

For those reasons, there are many scientists
Who have searched for its cause in the universe
Some say that the mass extinction was caused by a storm of comets
Which approached the earth regularly in a very long cycle
Others say it was caused by asteroids over 5 kilometres in diameter
Intersecting with the earth's orbit and so forth

Animals sustain their life in the environment in conjunction with plants
Plants grow where there is air and soil but seeds will not grow on a dead planet

As with water
The existence of plants is basic evidence that the earth is a living planet

Dinosaurs were rulers on the earth near the end of the Cretaceous period
They were becoming larger in size and proliferating in tremendous numbers
There was great fear that their appetite
Would consume all the plants on the earth

It meant that eventually other creatures could not be born or live on the earth
And the chances were that the earth itself
Would have perished in due course along with the dinosaurs

But it came to an end 65.5 million years ago
When a huge meteorite crashed on the earth...

It is very interesting to wonder
Whether this occurred in the universe by chance or through some kind of intention

Because dinosaurs have never reappeared on the earth since then
The fall of the meteorite changed the condition and environment of the earth
Ecologically, plant species became adapted
And mammals much smaller than dinosaurs appeared

Setting aside whether it was Nature's intention or not
The fact remains that the sudden changes in the earth's condition and environment
Due to the fall of a meteorite led to the creation of mankind

We could say that the human race came into existence through nature's preference
And during the 3 million years since the birth of mankind
This little mammal called man has survived by trying to live in harmony with nature

The earth no longer had to fear the dinosaurs' appetite
And a climate milder than ever before was provided for all creatures

At the First World Population Conference held in Rome back in 1954
The world population that was 2.5 billion at the time
Was predicted to increase up to 3.5 billion by 1980
But it actually had reached 4.4 billion

The world population that was 1 billion at the beginning of the twentieth century
Is expected to grow to around 10 billion during the twenty-first century

Man used to obtain food by gathering from nature
And then they learned how to grow, produce and preserve food
Agricultural and industrial revolutions have led to an amazing population increase

Man have been trying to change nature just for their own prosperity
As a result, many creatures have disappeared from the earth
And only mankind is continuing to multiply at an alarming rate

At present, mankind resemble the dinosaurs of the late Cretaceous period
Continuing to proliferate by feeding on many other creatures in order to survive

The dinosaurs were like cancer cells hindering the huge life form called the earth
Man may also be turning into cancer cells on the earth as if they were little dinosaurs
Due to their enormous population growth

65 million years ago, the earth accepted a remedy in an attempt to protect its life
A huge meteorite struck the surface of the earth
So that the rulers of the earth would change from dinosaurs to mammals
And its dream was entrusted to us mankind

Man is a mammal with a superior brain
And the volume of food supplied to man is incomparably smaller than dinosaurs

The earth was originally a huge living planet born through a planetesimal collision
When you think that its ultimate source of life exists in the universe
A remedy through a huge meteorite makes sense

Scientific progress has conflicted with nature throughout the history of mankind
But now we need to live in harmony with nature
Always caring and feeling gratitude for everything in nature including the universe
That has borne and cradled mankind's life

Even in academic studies such as science and physics
It is desirable to have not only cool-headed points of view but also attitudes of love

In August 1972, an American living in Wyoming named James Baker
Was using his 8 mm camera during a sightseeing tour
And by chance he filmed a huge meteorite
Weighing around 1,000 tons with a diameter of around 5 kilometres
That flew past just skimming the earth's atmosphere

The U.S. government announced this fact much later than Baker himself
If this huge meteorite had collided with the earth
Man would have perished before a storm of comets or intersecting asteroids came by

The earth's physical condition and environment also would have changed instantly
And a new species replacing mankind would have been born and prospered on earth
This might have been Nature's intention
Hoping that the new species would never repeat mankind's mistakes

Time Machine   *NO FUTURE*

In 1988

A report claiming that time machines were theoretically possible
Was announced in the U.S. and it caused a stir

                              It must be thrilling
                              To discuss the feasibility
                              Of mankind's dream of the time machine

However

If you look at it from another point of view
You will notice an unquestionable truth

                              This unquestionable truth
                              Is that time machines currently do not exist

In other words, if the theory is correct

And if it is going to be possible for mankind to create time machines in the future
Time machines would have already visited the present or the past
There should be an accomplished fact as such

But we

Have seen or heard about time machines
Only in novels and movies

                                                                             This fact

                                 Might lead us to the conclusion that
                     Mankind will never be able to obtain a time machine

    Scholars

Often determine matters only through calculations on paper
But it is often the case that when we look around for ourselves
Reality has already given us an answer

                                                  We might just be
                         Catching a glimpse of a blind spot in science

    Perhaps the report
On the time machine is symbolic of this fact

                Copernicus
                Announced his heliocentric theory in 1543

                                                                        Up till then

                                        Mankind continued to believe in the geocentric theory
                                    Though they were living in a reality that the earth was moving

                Perhaps man's intellect

            Cannot accept truth without argument
            Even when they face immutable facts

                                                                            The fact

                    That time machines do not exist allows us to arrive at a valuable hypothesis

                Which is that

            Whether time machines are theoretically possible or not
            We human beings can never actually get hold of one

In other words

Mankind cannot continue to exist until a time
When it would become scientifically possible to actually create time machines

If a scholar was convinced that
Time machines could be actualized in a hundred years' time

It would mean
Mankind would perish within the next hundred years

Even if it was five hundred or one thousand years later

It would mean
Mankind would not continue to exist until that time

This truth

Could be regarded as the length
Of mankind's existence using the time machine as a yardstick

This means

The more feasible time machines become
The sooner mankind's history will come to an end

Einstein may have discovered

The absolute feasibility of time machines
When he announced his theory of relativity

And at the same time

He might have realised that mankind's existence is drawing to a close
Because of the contradictory fact that time machines do not exist now

If just one person in the world

Witnessed mankind operating a time machine
It will prove mankind had obtained everlasting future...

Supposing UFOs

Are time machines
Then visitors from space like those depicted in Spielberg's film 'E.T.'

Could be the new form of life

Becoming the earth's leaders in the distant future after mankind perishes

This new simple life form

With a small body and a huge brain
Will apparently seem to have fewer physical needs and desires
In comparison to mankind

This could suggest

That after mankind perishes, the earth's new leader will be
A new form of life with qualities appropriate for living in harmony with nature

Dandelions *SPRING*

As you know, dandelions bloom in the hills in the springtime.
Of the 365 days of the year, dandelions bloom, let's say, for a month or so
Supposing I am a dandelion, then my life will end when I wither away
I won't know the sun on a hot summer's day, the autumn breeze or the winter snow
'Cause I'm a flower that blooms only in spring.
The earth has four seasons and the same season always comes around every 365 days.
And when the season comes, on the same hill where I used to grow
Another dandelion will bloom.
He won't know that I used to grow there just a year ago.
He'll poke his face out at the top of the hill for the first time and smell the young grass
He won't even think about when he's going to wither
He won't even know that there are four seasons and that it's spring then.
Just like me, who used to live in the mild weather of spring
He'll bloom on the soil that has warmed up after the snow melted
And will disappear before he's choked by the hot weather.

CHAPTER 7

As It Were Light
MISTY

The scent of young grass   Drifting clouds

Beneath the wind   My friend's voice calling me from afar

As It Were Light   *MISTY*

The midday sun
Its glorious rays of blessing
Lights everything it touches
In the dazzling brightness
We cannot see the sun
On the water
But can see glittering drops of light
The water
Reflects the surrounding landscape full of light
Beautifully and vividly
That is
When you feel joy
When everything seems to be shining beautifully
When you are so happy that you feel you do not need God
Even so
God is beside you
Blessing you each moment

The moon at night
Its delicate light
Only everything's silhouette
Are softly revealed
In the encompassing darkness
The quiet moonlight
Shines remarkably bright on the water
As it were reflected in a mirror
That is
When you are suffering
When your eyes are blurred with sadness
Hardly able to see even the things in front of you
When you are in need of God's help right away
You only need to wish for it
Then God will become what you can see forever
Which is the gentle moonlight
Watching over you

Beyond the Moment *SHADOW*

You think that this momentary incident
Is your entire life
And in your mind, you do not imagine beyond the moment

When you
Look at me as I am now
I might appear
Good, bad, wise or foolish
And you jump to a conclusion about me

Even if your impression of me is momentary
It will become eternal for you
And whether I change or not
You will engrave my momentary shadow in your mind forever

You will continue to look at my shadow forever even though it has disappeared
The same thing can be said of you

Right now you might be in distress
Though it could merely be your transient shadow
Assuming that it will go on forever
You might think it is beyond all salvation
You might even want to die

Your momentary shadow veils your shadowless future with darkness
Your shadow will change when you move
It will change even if you do not move

Your way of living will change your shadow
The flow of time will erase your shadow

The momentary shadow is born from you
And it is set free into Nature

Your past has already left your hands
And has been put into the hands of Nature

But you are living
Bound by your momentary shadow

Because
You know this moment
Has been carried from your past
And this moment
Is important as it will lead you to the future

To live in the moment
Is to become detached and to keep moving forward

Dream *STORY*

Do you know
Where your dream is heading for?

Though your dream should be what you create yourself
And you are supposed to be the author of your dream

Like a hero who is not aware of the story
In your dream, you drift between joy and sorrow

Perhaps your reality is the same as your dream

Though your life
Should be what you create yourself
And you should be able to portray your own life story

Like a hero who cannot grasp the story
In reality you may drift between joy and sorrow

Your dreams
Are born from your memories

There is always a cause for every result
And each result becomes the next cause

Your present is linked like a piece of thread
Between your past and future

Your present is the result of your past
Your future will be the extension of your present

If you want to know your present
You should recollect your past

If you want to know your future
You should take a look at your present

In doing so
You will no longer drift between joy and sorrow in reality
Like a hero in a dream who cannot grasp the story

But you will become the author of your own life and lead a truly fruitful life

Bunch of Grapes *A PIECE OF HEART*

Your heart
Like a bunch of grapes
Tastes of grapes growing on the vine of your life

Your heart
Does not just have a single thought
But it is a collection of several thoughts

As the vine grows
Grapes ripen

When you were a child
Your grapes were sour
And your heart could be understood clearly

But now
Your bunch of grapes
Bears grapes of various flavours

When people eat your grapes
Some say it is delicious and some say it is not

As for yourself
You do not even know the taste of your own grapes

But
You cherish the grapes that others enjoy

You as an infant
Have not borne fruit yet

So no one
Tries to eat your grapes

But
They hope you will become a rich and delicious bunch of grapes

You as a boy
Are yet an unripe bunch of grapes
No one will blame you for tasting bitter

You as a young man
Have become a sweet-and-sour bunch of grapes

After a bite
People decide to wait for you to ripen a bit more

You as a grown man
Have become a bunch of ripe grapes

People
Do not hesitate to have big mouthfuls
And you might be blamed if there is a grape that tasted bad

Many seasons
Have passed and you have borne grapes with each cycle

Seasons have gone by
Your vines have grown old
Grapes no longer grow and people no longer gather around you

You
Are all alone
Remembering the lush grapes you used to produce

Now
For you
Every grape tastes good

When winter comes
You will wither and decay
Return to soil and lose even your memories

After a few summers

In the place
Where you used to be
The seeds of grapes
Fallen from your vines had grown into large grapevines unnoticed

And on it
Many rich bunches of grapes were growing

『神のみる夢』刊行によせて

　今から5年程前になるだろうか。著者、合田和厚氏に出逢ったのは……。
　それ以来、毎月のように人々を力づけ、なぐさめ、心の支えとなった講話の数々。氏の静かな口調で語られる心の話、魂の話、愛の話、神の話、宇宙の話等が、ごく普通の当り前の話題として耳に入ってくるのはなぜだろう。それは、誰もが持っている先入観や偏見を超えて、言葉が心そのものに訴えかけてくるからに違いない。大切にとどめておきたいたくさんの言葉、それが耳にした次の瞬間には虚空へ消えてしまうのを、私はいつも心惜しく感じていた。

　しかし、今は一冊の本が私の手元にある。長い間、待ち望んでいた本がついに出版される。あの柔らかな口調で述べられた深遠な話が本になる。私を感動させた語りも、涙させた一説も本になる。心引き締まる未来への提言も本になる。

　深夜、静まりかえった部屋で分厚い原稿を手にすると、クリーム色のワープロ用紙に打ち出された文字が急に生き生きと感じられて、体温を持っているかのように錯覚してしまう。目で辿る言葉の一つひとつが私の中に入ると、立体的な情景へと変化していく。一瞬にして言葉の持つ波紋が心の奥底にまで広がり、私は言い表す事の出来ない感動でいっぱいになる。
　読み進むうちに、すっかり引き込まれてしまい、一節毎に変化する場面で様々な役柄を演じているような気持ちになっていく。

　氏の天才的インスピレーションによって書き上げられたこの「神のみる夢」には個人的・社会的・宗教的・精神的・宇宙的・全ての問題に対する答えが、驚く程明確に記されている。氏は各個人が幸福になる事を常に第一と考えていますが、その為には、人間に関わる様々なファクターが良い方向へ向かう事が必要であると述べているに違いないのです。現代は地球的視野から見た思いやり、宇宙的規模の愛という考え方を必要とする時代であるのかも

知れません。まさしく人類は、第6章の「タンポポ　SPRING」の何も知らずに咲くタンポポそのものなのかも知れません。その為筆者は、私の心のスクリーンに、微細な粒子から広大な宇宙までの全てを映して見せたのです。

　1頁目から始まった心の旅は、自分の一生をたった数時間で辿ってしまったような緊張と驚きの連続。そして、辿り着いたのは満ち足りた〔今〕という瞬間だった。「人はなぜ生まれ、愛し、死んでいくのか」誰もが投げかける問いかけを無言のまま大きな手のひらで包んでくれた。そんな安堵感でいっぱいになる。しんと静まりかえった夜更け、頁をめくる音が止まった時、言葉という枠は次々と砕けちり瑞々しいまでの生命力だけが確かな手応えとして残されていた。ちょうど桜の花が散った時のように、私の心の中には散ったばかりの花の生命を受け継いだ花びらが、震えながらも幾重にも重なっていく。

　数時間後、原稿を読み終えてふと気が付く、先程の花びらは跡形もなく消え去っていた。夢を見ていたのだろうか。春の暖かさに包まれた私は、これからあるがままに生きていけそうな幸福な気持ちでいっぱいだった。

1988年9月1日

On the Publication of *The Dreams of God*

It was around five years ago that I got to know Mr. Yasuhiro Goda. Ever since, I have attended his monthly lectures, at which he has given encouragement, comfort and mental support to many people by providing food for thought. In a quiet tone, he talks about our mind and soul, love, God, the universe and so forth, and I have been wondering why his words sounded so natural and obvious. It must be because they speak directly to our hearts, beyond preconceptions and biases that we all have. I always felt frustrated when the things he said in abundance, which I cherished and wanted to retain, vanished into thin air right after I heard them.

However, now I have a book with me. It is the book that I have been looking forward to for a long time and it will be published at last. The profound lectures that Mr. Goda had given us in his soft tone have been compiled into a book. His stories that touched my heart and his passages that made me cry have become a book. His sobering visions of the future are also written in the book.

Late at night, in a quite room, I picked up the thick manuscript of the book and the letters that were printed on a cream-colored printing paper suddenly became vibrant and I had an illusion that the words were alive. Each word that I followed with my eyes turned into stereoscopic scenes when they entered my mind. The repercussions of his words instantly appealed to me deep inside and I became filled with a sensation beyond explanation.

As I read on, I was completely drawn into the book and felt as if was playing various characters as the scenes changed in each passage.

The Dreams of God, which is a collection of poems that Mr. Goda has written with his gifted inspiration, provides stunningly explicit answers to various questions at personal, social, religious, spiritual, cosmic and all other levels. He puts each person's happiness first, and without doubt he is saying that in order to be happy, various factors related to mankind have to go in the right direction. One might say that in today's world, we are required to think about compassion with a global perspective and love on a cosmic scale. Human beings might be exactly like the dandelions blossoming unconsciously in the poem 'Dandelions *SPRING*' in Chapter 6. That is why the author has helped me project on the screen inside my mind everything ranging from microscopic particles to the vast universe.

From the very first page, I had set out on a spiritual journey, through which I experienced tension and astonishment one after another as though I had gone through my lifetime in just a few hours. In the end, I arrived at the blissful state of existing in the moment. "Why do we come into the world, experience love and then die?"—–most of us have probably asked this question and Mr. Goda has tacitly implied the answers in an all-encompassing way. That must be why I was filled with a sense of relief. In the middle of the night, when all was silent, I stopped flipping the manuscript paper and the frames set by words crumbled one after another, leaving behind only refreshing life force that was perceptible. Just like the petals of cherry blossoms falling, in my mind, the petals, which had succeeded the life of the flower that had just fallen, pile up layer upon layer while they are still quivering.

A few hours later, when I had read through the manuscript, I realized that the heap of petals had disappeared, leaving no trace whatsoever. Perhaps I was dreaming. Wrapped in the warm spring air, my heart was full of happiness as I felt that I could lead my life as it is.

September 1, 1988

あとがきにかえて　*Pocketful of Rainbows*

　平成元年に1冊目の著作集『神のみる夢』を出版してから、長く書き綴っていた詩作を『神のくちづけ』と題して上梓することととなり、『神のみる夢』も時をあわせて新たに刊行するはこびとなりました。

『神のみる夢』を以前から読まれていた方、今回はじめて読まれる方への感謝をこめて新たなイメージの装丁となり、英訳を入れています。

　この2冊の本の詩の1つ1つが　雨上がりの虹のように貴方の心をときめかせ、気持ちのいい風がそっと貴方に吹いてきますように。

　心からの祈りをこめて。

2017年1月
合田 和厚

In Place of an Afterward   *Pocketful of Rainbows*

I am privileged to publish tne newly edited version of *The Dreams of God*, which was first published in 1988, as well *The Kiss of God*, which is a collection of poems I have written for many years since then.

The Dreams of God has been bound with a new image and this time it includes English translation, as a way for me to express gratitude to those who have read the existing versions and also to those who will be reading it for the first time.

I hope that each and every poem in the two collections will make your heart flutter like when you see a rainbow across the sky after the heavy rain and that you will be caressed by a pleasant breeze.

With prayers from my heart,

January 2017
Yasuhiro Goda

神のみる夢

2017年1月28日　第1刷発行

著者　合田和厚

発行所　株式会社マインドカルチャーセンター
〒145-0071　東京都大田区田園調布2-8-13-101
電話　03（3721）6365
振替　00130-9-137973
印刷・製本　株式会社東京印書館
英訳　角田美知代
NDC920
Ⓒ 2017 Yasuhiro Goda
Published by Mind Culture Center Co., Ltd. Printed in Japan
ISBN978-4-944017-08-9
乱丁本・落丁本は小社負担でおとりかえいたします。

この本は平成元年刊行の『神のみる夢』（マインドカルチャーセンター）に英訳を付した新装版です。

本書のコピー、スキャン、デジタル化等の無断複製は著作権法上での例外を除き禁じられています。本書を代行業者等の第三者に依頼してスキャンやデジタル化することは、たとえ個人や家庭内での利用であっても一切認められておりません。